THE CASE

of the

CAMBRIDGE
MUMMY

D0493648

Also by Joan Lennon and published by Catnip:
The Case of the London Dragonfish
The Case of the Glasgow Ghoul

And for younger readers:
The Ferret Princess
Wag and the King
The Mucker's Tale

A SLIGHTLY JONES MYSTERY

THE CASE

of the

CAMBRIDGE MUMMY

JOAN LENNON

Catnip

CATNIP BOOKS
Published by Catnip Publishing Ltd
14 Greville Street
London
EC1N 8SB

This edition first published 2012

3 5 7 9 10 8 6 4 2

Text copyright © Joan Lennon, 2012
The moral right of the author has been asserted.

Cover design by Mandy Norman
Cover illustration by Shane Clester

A CIP catalogue record for this book is available from the British Library.

ISBN 978-1-84647-1407

Printed in Poland

www.catnippublishing.co.uk

Everybody's heard of Florence Nightingale
and David Livingstone. These books are dedicated
to the Victorian heroes and heroines who
aren't so famous!

This one is for John Kemp Starley –
Inventor of the Safety Bicycle

(As the campaigner for Votes for Women,
Susan B. Anthony, said in 1896: 'Let me tell you
what I think of bicycling. I think it has done more
to emancipate women than anything else in the
world . . . I stand and rejoice every time I see
a woman ride by on a wheel.')

CONTENTS

Chapter One:
The Watcher in the Tower

'**G**oodbye! Goodbye! See you next term! Have a good Christmas! Love to your parents!'

A curtain twitched in the tower as the cries of departing students rang out in the cold air. Someone was watching as the young women left. Watching as the short winter day ended, and darkness flowed across the college grounds. The watcher welcomed the dark. She felt it creeping into deserted lecture halls and bedrooms, chapel and laboratory and dining hall and library. She felt it climb the tower stairs and fill the room.

She let the curtain drop. Behind her, someone stirred restlessly.

'Is it time yet?' Her companion's voice was fretful.

'Not long, Celestial One,' soothed the watcher. 'Soon it will be time.'

The owner of the querulous voice seemed unable to keep still. She paced about the room like a caged animal. As she walked, her feet raised puffs of a strange scent out of the heavy carpet – too sweet to be pleasant, with an edge that caught at the throat and irritated the eyes. The fretful murmuring continued.

'It *must* be time! They are gone, with their pointless, noisy, human concerns. My Lord Anubis grows impatient for my prayers. I order you to prepare the way!'

The watcher smiled, a small secret smile.

'Yes, my queen. Of course. It shall be as you wish . . .'

CHAPTER TWO:
Curses and High Collars

Slightly Jones clattered down the stairs singing, 'Today's the day! Today's the day!' She skidded to a halt at the kitchen door, took one look at Matthew Bone, and burst out laughing.

Anything *less* like the Matthew she'd first met – Matthew the street boy, Matthew the pickpocket, Matthew the disreputable ragamuffin know-it-all – would be hard to imagine. His hair had been trimmed and washed and plastered to his head with macassar oil, and his face scrubbed to within an inch of its life. He was wearing a pair of boots so fiercely shined they practically sparkled, a tweed suit, a high, stiff, brilliantly white collar, and a big proud smirk on his face.

'What . . . *do* you . . . look like?!' Slightly hiccupped.

Miss Sally Forth put her head on one side and considered Matthew. 'I think he looks *lovely*,' she said.

But that was no surprise, since she was the one who'd chosen the pickpocket's new clothes. He was her star expert – he was coming to Cambridge to help her write a chapter on London slang for her friend's new book, and she was determined he would do her proud! She'd also put Matthew on a crash course in how to behave in company, based on the book *Manners for Little Ladies and Gentleman* by Mrs W. Ebenezer.

Teacher's pet! thought Slightly. *Of course* she *thinks he looks lovely!*

'What does he look like?' Granny Tonic said sternly. 'He looks like a well dressed young gentleman, who is going on the train with us to Cambridge University, where he will be of great use to Miss Forth and her friend in their linguistic research. And *you*, Slightly, are acting like a very rude little girl who could do with some lessons from Mrs Ebenezer's book herself!'

Oh-oh – better get a grip, Slightly, she told herself. *I will not laugh . . . I will not laugh . . .* She clamped her hand to her mouth and screwed her eyes shut and swallowed hard. *There. I'm in control. I'm in control . . .*

She opened her eyes, took another look at Matthew and got as far as, 'You're right – of course – Matthew, you really *do* look lovely!' before dissolving into giggles again.

Matthew growled. Slightly saw his fingers twitch and guessed he was seriously considering pulling her red curls for her. Granny must have noticed too, and quickly got between them before he could lunge.

'That's enough!' she said to them both. 'Matthew, what does Mrs W. Ebenezer say about pulling hair?'

'My apologies, Miss Tonic,' said Matthew, bowing carefully, with one eye on Miss Forth to see if he was getting it right. 'Mrs Ebenezer quite discourages it.' Miss Forth gave him an encouraging nod. Matthew puffed up like a smug toad, crossed his eyes at Slightly and added in a whisper, 'Besides, in a bird's nest like that who knows *what* you might find!'

She had already started to stick her tongue out at him when she realised Granny was watching with a beady eye.

Oh-oh.

'Sorry, Granny,' she muttered.

Slightly called Granny Tonic 'Granny' even though she wasn't really Slightly's grandmother. She was, in fact, her mother's aunt – which meant that she was really Slightly's great-aunt. But ever since Slightly had come to live at Limpopo House, after her parents died, she'd called Granny 'Granny' and nothing else. It was just the way it was.

Now Granny gave her a fierce look. It seemed a good idea to behave like a model young lady, at least for the moment.

'Right,' said Granny. 'That's that. Now, do we have everything? Are we ready to go?'

At this, everybody in the room began to talk and give advice and look about for luggage and parcels and baskets and anything else that might have been forgotten and then discovered to be the one thing they needed, when they'd already left for Cambridge and it was too late.

'We must take plenty of warm woolly mittens and mufflers,' shrilled Miss Forth. 'The wind off the Fens comes all the way from Siberia!'

Granny and Slightly exchanged glances. Miss Forth was wonderful at anything to do with languages, but sometimes she could be a bit hazy on geography.

Slightly checked that she had her detecting notebook and her silver propelling pencil safely in her pocket, and then stood back to watch the chaos with a happy smile on her face.

All the lodgers of Limpopo House were there that morning. Mr Thurgood had just come in from his job as night watchman at London's fine Natural History Museum. He was trying to tell Miss Forth what was going to happen next in the very exciting book he was writing. (Every morning he came home with more amazing ideas, concocted as he walked about in the dark building with only dinosaur bones and stuffed elephants to keep him company.) Mr Westerly, his magnificent moustache bristling with excitement, was giving Granny advice on the most beautiful buildings in Cambridge, why she *must* see them, who had built them, and when. He was a painter and passionate about such things. And Mr Gentler was quietly making some sandwiches for them to eat on the train. He was slicing ham and gherkins the way he did everything – in time to the tune inside his head. He caught Slightly's eye and gave her an encouraging wink.

The three gentlemen lodgers were going to be staying put over Christmas, while Slightly, Granny Tonic, Miss Forth and Matthew went to Cambridge. They would be looking after Limpopo House and, in particular, Miss Forth's elderly cat,

Cleopatra. Slightly could see her crouched under the kitchen table, lashing her tail and growling angrily. Cleopatra did not approve of all the noise and fuss. At the last moment, her mistress tried to get her to come and say goodbye properly, only to be scratched for her trouble.

'Oww!'

'Don't worry – she'll be fine with us!' said Mr Gentler.

'We'll take good care of her – you know we will!' said Mr Westerly.

'Goodbye! Goodbye!' they all cried.

They seem surprisingly cheerful, thought Slightly. *You'd think they'd be sad, being left behind when there's a mystery to be solved, with a mummy and a curse and EVERYTHING!* And then she forgot all about them, and leaned forward in the hansom cab, trying to peer out both windows at once.

Matthew, who had handed them into the cab, muttering 'Ladies first . . . ladies first . . .' now sat with his back to the horse. He looked gentlemanly for a full thirty seconds before he gave up and started jostling Slightly for the best views.

It was a cold morning, and the London street-sellers were out in force, crying their wares – hot sheep's trotters and roasted chestnuts, baked potatoes and pickled whelks and boiled eels. The mud in the street had a film of ice over it. Those who could afford it were wearing mufflers and gloves and hats, but Slightly saw more than one poor street cleaner whose feet were bare and blue.

'London don't half look different from inside a cab!' Matthew said. He knew the city better than Slightly did, as he never tired of telling her. He'd lived on the streets and off his wits for his whole life, picking pockets, holding horses, guiding rich Londoners through the awful fogs that descended on the capital with dismal regularity. Sometimes she felt sorry for him because of his hard life, but then he'd open his mouth and she'd just get irritated all over again. When she was solving the Case of the London Dragonfish in the Natural History Museum, he'd helped Slightly with her detecting – but he didn't know *everything*!

'I've never been on a Mary Blaine before,' he admitted as they pulled into King's Cross Station.

'A what?' said Miss Forth.

'A train.'

'Oh, a train. Mary Blaine, train. I'll just make a note of that . . .'

'Plenty more where that came from!' said Matthew smugly.

'This is just a *short* journey,' Slightly said, hoping to bring him down a peg or two. She'd taken the *long* train trip all the way north to Scotland, where she'd solved the remarkable Case of the Glasgow Ghoul. Thankfully, Matthew hadn't been involved with that. Slightly sighed. She wasn't sure she was going to be able to stand him for the length of a train ride, let alone having him butting in on this new and wonderfully twisty mystery right over Christmas!

As they settled into their carriage and the train pulled out of the station, Matthew hogged the window, exclaiming at everything they passed. Slightly pulled out her detecting notebook and did her best to ignore him. And Granny and Miss Forth? Well, even though the ride to Cambridge was only going to take a few hours, *they* were barely out of London before they were snoring genteelly in opposite corners of the carriage.

Slightly looked over at them. *What is it about trains that always put grown-ups to sleep?* she wondered. *It's just another mystery,* she decided and turned to her notes on the new case.

The first ones had been scribbled fast while Miss Forth was reading out her friend's letter, so they were a bit confusing.

Mellifluous Sprottle (!) Mr Entwhistle
Fitzwilliam Museum → Egyptian
Department → VANDALISM! →
curse . . . mummy . . . mystery . . .

But now she turned to a fresh page, unscrewed her propelling pencil and began with a proper title:

The Case of the Cambridge Mummy

A good name for a case was always an excellent place to start, she felt. From there, a good detective laid out all her information:

Where? The Egyptian Department at the
Fitzwilliam Museum in Cambridge.

When? Since the museum acquired a beautiful
Egyptian necklace with a colourful history – it is
said to be cursed! Ghastly glowing mummy seen
stalking museum corridors after dark!

What is the crime? Priceless Egyptian artefacts
are being mysteriously smashed.

It made Slightly feel sick. Fragile, wonderful objects that had managed to last all those thousands of years were now being callously, pointlessly, deliberately destroyed. Miss Sprottle's letter told of priceless statues, precious papyrus covered in hieroglyphs, jars for holding bits of mummified bodies, delicate glass vases – ancient objects vandalised beyond repair.

How? Nobody knows!

Who is involved? Miss Mellifluous Sprottle (Miss Forth's linguistic friend) and her fiancé Mr Edward Entwhistle (head of the Egyptian Department at the Fitzwilliam)

Suspects so far. . .

Slightly looked at her list. It wasn't very satisfactory.

1. Mr Entwhistle – but why would he smash treasures in his own department?
2. Miss Sprottle – but why would she smash treasures in her own fiancé's department?
3. The mummy . . .

Mummies and curses – Slightly knew all about

these sorts of things from reading Penny Dreadfuls (which she did in secret, since Granny did *not* approve). People who disturbed the sacred rest of the dead in those publications would invariably meet a terrible fate, usually involving being buried alive or having their insides removed in some particularly unpleasant fashion. She'd never read a story where the curse resulted in vandalism, though . . . but, she reminded herself firmly, the stories in the Penny Dreadfuls were *fiction*.

And the curse of the mummy's necklace was better than any made-up story. As Miss Sprottle had reminded them in her letter, Egypt's history was long and sometimes violent. There were hundreds of years when the country was divided between many kingdoms, each fighting the next, each trying to expand by conquest.

She wrote Miss Sprottle's tale out it in full, just as she remembered it from the letter . . .

There once was a powerful pharaoh, who in the course of his various campaigns succeeded in vanquishing the armies of a neighbouring queen. When she was ordered to come before her conqueror, the queen decked herself out in her finest linen, adorned her hair and put on the

*most valuable necklace she owned – a wonder of
gold and precious stones – workmanship such as
the world had never seen. Then she took a slow-
acting poison and, head held high, she walked
into the court of the conqueror . . .*

Granny and Miss Forth slept peacefully and Matthew
watched, engrossed, as the wintery countryside
flashed by, but Slightly was far away, in a hot land
long, long ago.

*The conquered queen took care to stand where
the light would fall on the necklace, the glittering
gold and the pools of brilliant colour. She made
sure that everyone there could see the treasure she
wore around her neck, knowing that to see it was
to desire it.*

Slightly could picture the scene as clearly as if it were
happening right there in front of her.

*And then she spoke these words:
'You who are so mighty, know that I have
cursed this necklace with my dying breath. I will
die and be forgotten, but my curse will not die.*

It will live on, long after I am dust. But the one who takes this necklace will never rest. In life, in death, you will know no peace. You will walk the world and only destruction will follow in your footsteps.'

Then she closed her lips and fell down dead at the foot of the pharaoh.

Impressed in spite of all his power, the pharaoh ordered the queen and her necklace to be consigned to the fire at once. He wanted none of her curse – but the pharaoh's consort had also seen the necklace, and she desired it more than anything else. She persuaded the pharaoh that the dead queen's speech was all just meaningless words – that if he really loved her, he would give her this little thing – that he was so powerful, nothing could touch him – anything and everything she could think of to make him do what she wanted.

Slightly knew without being told that he would give in. It was inevitable.

The very day the pharaoh's consort put the beautiful cursed necklace round her own neck was the day that marked the beginning of the end. The pharaoh started to lose in battle – the nations he had already conquered rose up against him – famine and plague afflicted his people. One by one, his children succumbed and at last the consort herself died miserably. She was made into a mummy and laid into the stone tomb cut for her in a hidden place. The years passed, and she and the pharaoh and the curse were forgotten.

Then, centuries later, the tomb was discovered by archaeologists. However, when they entered, no mummy was found! Only the necklace remained, lying in the sarcophagus with a papyrus on which the story of the curse was written in hieroglyphs, a papyrus so dried out with age that it fell into dust as soon as the archaeologists read it . . .

Slightly sighed. Of course this made no sense to a detective like her. Where was the mummy? If grave robbers had gone to all the trouble of stealing a mummy, they wouldn't go and leave a priceless necklace behind!

There was one last thing to write. One last problem . . .

Miss Sprottle wants Miss Forth to write a chapter on London slang for her book, so Matthew's been invited to Cambridge too. Now there's a REAL curse!

'Oi – that's my name!'

Slightly jumped so hard she bit her tongue. Matthew was leaning over her shoulder, pointing at her notebook.

'Right there – see?! What're you saying about me then?'

Slightly slammed her notebook shut and growled, 'I'm saying you're a pest and a nuisance – and didn't anyone ever tell you it's rude to read somebody else's private notebook?!'

Matthew grinned. 'Old Mrs Ebenezer hasn't said a dicky bird about notebooks – just letters and messages.'

'Well, here's a message for *you* – STAY OUT OF MY NOTEBOOK!'

Matthew's grin just got broader. 'Oh, why is that – is it full of how much you love me? Or no – I know – I bet it's full of how scared you are of this Cambridge Mummy! Admit it – you're scared stiff!'

Slightly snorted. 'Nobody believes in mummies, stupid.'

'The guards at the Museum do, so stupid yourself! They've *seen* it! Walking the corridors, strange and glowing, there one second and then the next, suddenly, it vanishes. That's who's smashing up the artefacts, you mark my words. That mummy what vanished out of the tomb has shown up, is toddling about the place and doing cursed things right, left and centre. Now no one wants to come to work any more, is what Miss Forth says.'

'Can you *hear* yourself?!' Slightly squawked. 'How do you think a mummy could get all the way from Egypt in Africa to Cambridge in England? Take a boat? Travel on the train? Can't you just see it coming up to the ticket office and saying, "One to England, if you please." In ancient Egyptian!'

By the time she finished her voice was *much* louder than Mrs W. Ebenezer would have called polite. Granny and Miss Forth stirred.

'Oh! Oh, I think I must have . . .' Miss Forth looked about her bemused, and then tidied her hair. She didn't really need to, Slightly noticed with a sigh. *How does she manage to stay so neat? When I'm grown up, will I be tidy?* She hoped so, but thought probably not.

'Nearly there,' said Granny with a carefully covered yawn.

'What's this Cambridge place like, Miss Forth?' asked Matthew, going all polite and gentlemanly again.

'Oh, quite a sleepy place – some lovely old buildings, and in the summer you can go boating on the river. When I was there last I was taken punting – that's what they call it – by such a pleasant young man. I wore a straw hat with lilac-coloured ribbons.' She had a strangely goopy expression on her face as she remembered.

Slightly tried not to giggle and Matthew looked at her and crossed his eyes, then lowered the window and leaned out so far his new boots left the floor. None of them could hear what he was saying.

Granny tugged on his jacket. 'Matthew, come back in here at once! I'm not having you falling on your head on the train tracks. It's bad manners!'

Matthew landed back on his boots instead, turned and yelped something Mrs W. Ebenezer definitely would not have approved of.

'Blimey O'Riley!' he cried, eyes shining. 'It's a riot!'

CHAPTER THREE:
Riots and Riders

Slightly tried to get *her* head out of the window too. 'What? Shove over – I can't see!'

Granny promptly pulled both Matthew and Slightly back and leaned out herself.

'Good heavens!' she muttered.

But it was too late to do anything – the train was already slowing at the platform. Though you couldn't really *see* the platform – it was completely hidden by a seething, jostling crowd of young men, a mass of straw boater hats and college scarves.

They were as rowdy as squabbling gulls,

shouting, pushing past each other to get to friends, punching each others' shoulders.

'I'm sure it's nothing to worry about . . . just the students, going home for the holidays!' Miss Forth had to shout to be heard over the tumult.

Then it got even louder! Somebody in the crowd started singing a song about how wonderful his particular college was and then somebody else began to shout out a rival anthem, and soon they were all bellowing different tunes at the top of their lungs.

Sleepy Cambridge, my foot! thought Slightly.

'Well,' shouted Granny, pushing her hat firmly down on her head. 'This is our stop and this is where we're getting out. They certainly won't be interested in *us*!'

But she was wrong. The moment Granny started to struggle with the carriage door, there was a cry of 'Heads up, lads! Ladies in distress!' and dozens of students leapt into action.

''Ere – get off 'em!' cried Matthew, but he was swept aside. Granny, Miss Forth, Slightly and their luggage were enthusiastically dragged from the train – they were going to be escorted, whether they wanted to be or not.

'Mind out – ladies coming through – here, get out of the way!'

'Let go of my granny!' yelled Slightly. She could hear Miss Forth going 'Oh! Oh!' somewhere behind her – she tried to turn back, but all she could see were overcoats and manic grins –

'Matthew?' she yelled. 'Where's Matthew?'

And then a shout went up – 'The train! The train's leaving!' With a whoop and a laugh their escort turned tail and ran, leaving the visitors from London in the Cambridge station entrance hall, as dishevelled and breathless as if they'd been cast ashore by a boisterous sea.

'Well! My goodness! I never ... It certainly wasn't like this the last time I was here!' twittered Miss Forth, all agitated.

'I could have robbed that lot blind if it weren't for me being on gentlemanly behaviour,' muttered Matthew mournfully as he came up behind them.

'But where is Miss Sprottle?' said Slightly. 'Isn't she meant to be meeting us?'

They gathered up their belongings and went out onto the street. There was no sign of anyone to meet them.

Miss Forth peered about anxiously. 'Oh dear – I can't imagine what has happened. Mellifluous is normally such a punctual person!'

'We'll take a cab,' Granny soothed her. 'The driver

is sure to know where Girton College is. Matthew, if you'd nip down the street and hail us one . . .'

But as Matthew started down the steps, Slightly grabbed his arm and dragged him back again.

'Oi! That hurt!' he exclaimed.

'Look!' said Slightly, pointing. 'Could *that* be Miss Sprottle?'

A figure wearing voluminous bloomers, a short tailored jacket, with her hair coming down and her hat tilted dangerously over one ear, was peddling furiously towards them – on a bicycle!

'Mellifluous!' cried Miss Forth.

Miss Sprottle smiled and waved, causing her bicycle to wobble wildly. As if by magic, several porters appeared from the train station, calling out, 'Careful, Miss! Are you all right? Did you have any trouble, Miss?' They crowded around her as she came to an abrupt stop at the bottom of the steps and climbed off her machine.

'I'm fine – don't worry – only a little trouble, thank you – the boys are all a bit overexcited, because of going home for the holidays.' And she pushed her hat back up onto the top of her head and gave Miss Forth a big hug. 'My dear Sally – it's wonderful to see you again. It's been far too long. Not since we sat in the back of Miss Pringle's class and read the dictionary when we should have been learning our times tables!'

Slightly looked at the two with interest. They made quite a picture – Miss Forth so neat and tidy, dressed in her very proper travelling outfit, and Miss Sprottle, so modern and exciting in her bicycling bloomers and boater hat – and her hair! *Her hair's as messy as mine!* thought Slightly in amazement.

'These your visitors, Miss? We'll get you a cab now, shall we?' said the head porter in a fatherly fashion. 'We can have the luggage and Peggy sent on by wagon.'

'That would be splendid. Thank you very much.' Miss Sprottle beamed at them all, and they all beamed back. As the carriage and wagon were called for she explained in a low voice to her visitors. 'I named my bicycle Pegasus but the porters insist on referring to her as Peggy. They have a kind of proprietary interest in keeping me from an untimely accidental death – I've written an entire chapter about their slang, and I think they fear to lose their moment of fame if I'm not able to finish my book because of some terrible bicycling disaster!'

She pinned an escaping lock of hair somewhat haphazardly back into place and held out her hand to Granny.

'You must be Miss Tonic. I'm so pleased to meet you. My good friend Sally has told me so much about you. And this fine gentleman must be Master Bone. I look forward to working with you, sir.' She turned to Slightly. 'And this is surely Miss Jones. I had no idea you were so young.'

Slightly's heart sank. *Here we go again*, she thought glumly. *Little girls can't be detectives, blah blah blah. You'd think a lady linguist would be more modern!*

And, as it turned out, Miss Sprottle *was*.

'This is excellent,' she continued with a big beaming smile. 'Young minds are so much more elastic. I'm sure you will see many things in this case, my dear, that older, stiffer brains will have completely missed.'

Slightly decided right then and there that Mellifluous Sprottle was a wise and delightful woman.

Sooner than she would have thought possible, the porters were handing them into a cab. Matthew had volunteered to follow on with the luggage. He suddenly looked quite small, standing there on the steps to the station in his rather rumpled finery. Slightly felt a little sorry for him. It was an uncomfortable feeling . . .

'Don't let anybody nick our bags,' she called out to him.

He immediately perked up. 'Like to see 'em try!' he shouted back cockily.

Slightly grinned and leaned back on the seat.

The short winter afternoon was almost over as the cab trundled through the streets of the ancient town. They passed the gas lighter at his work, and the blossoms of brightness he left behind lit up colleges and chapels of yellow brick and fine stone, and then a marketplace full of canopied stalls, still doing brisk business by torchlight. The streets were full of overexcited students, bustling about on last-minute errands before dispersing for the holidays.

'They're all men, aren't they,' said Slightly.

'Good fellows, every one,' said Miss Sprottle kindly. 'It's taking them a little while to get used to the idea of women studying and working and getting their university degrees, the way they do – but it won't be long! Any day now and all this silly resistance will be over.'

'Is it true what I heard,' said Miss Forth anxiously, 'that the male students hung a straw effigy of a lady on a bicycle out of a second storey window in the centre of town when it was proposed that female students be given degrees? And then tore her to bits in celebration when the idea was defeated?'

'Well . . . yes. But don't worry. It was just high spirits, my dear, just high spirits.'

A bit more than THAT! thought Slightly.

Granny looked troubled, and when a male voice shouted suddenly close to the cab, Miss Forth jumped visibly. The young man was only trying to attract the attention of his friends across the road, however, and soon the cab was crossing over the River Cam and on into a quieter part of town. There were fewer and fewer buildings here and more and more flat, open countryside, and then, at last, the cab pulled up at an ornate gate.

'We're here,' cried Miss Sprottle. 'Welcome to Girton College!'

An older man hurried out of the gatehouse and opened the gates for them.

'Thank you, Mr Peters,' Miss Sprottle called through the window.

He peered into the cab. 'That you, Miss Sprottle? Where's your infernal machine, then?'

'It's coming, Mr Peters, don't you worry! The lad who'll be staying with you and Mrs Peters is bringing it with him on the station wagon. He'll be here soon.'

'Well, and that's fine. My missus has supper hot and ready for him. Shall I check to see there's nothing needs fixing on that Peggy of yours, though?'

'No, many thanks, Mr Peters . . .' He looked so disappointed that she quickly added, ' . . . but she could surely do with a good clean, if you'd be so kind?'

With a satisfied grin on his face, Mr Peters waved the cab on up the drive towards a dark, imposing building with a square tower at the centre. For a brief moment Slightly saw a light flickering in a window at the top, and then it abruptly blinked out as they passed underneath an archway and into the courtyard beyond.

'Come in, come in!'

Servants bustled about with lanterns, for it was completely dark now. Slightly and the others were hurried into the library, a warm, book-lined room with a cheerful fire blazing and comfortable chairs beckoning. They were more than a little shabby, and the table where a steaming supper was laid must have doubled as a work desk, for it was marked with ink stains. Slightly felt strangely at home.

'Are we the only residents, Miss Sprottle?' asked Granny.

'Practically,' she replied, nodding her head and losing another hairpin. 'The only others staying over the holiday are Miss Amberleigh and her assistant

Miss Ponsonby. They must be working late again this evening.' Slightly noticed Miss Sprottle's smiley face fall, but then she gave herself a shake and went on. 'Miss Amberleigh – she prefers to be called Professor Amberleigh, though of course the university does not believe in lady professors – is our expert in ancient civilizations. And Miss Ponsonby is a student but also a skilled restorer. Sadly, her abilities have been much in demand – because of this terrible mystery – these senseless acts . . . ' She shook her head sadly, then remembered her guests and cried, 'But please – eat! I know you must be hungry!'

They did not need more urging, and set to with a good will.

'We normally eat in the dining hall, of course,' said Miss Sprottle, 'but with the students gone I thought this was cosier. Tomorrow I can show you round the college – the chapel and the lecture halls and our laboratory – we're ever so proud of that.'

But Slightly was more interested in getting down to detecting. 'Please, Miss Sprottle, could we not go to the Museum first?'

'Yes! Yes, indeed. In fact, Miss Amberleigh is giving a public lecture there tomorrow. She's terribly knowledgeable about the Egyptian artefacts. Perhaps you might like to attend?'

Slightly nodded. Anything to get to the scene of the crimes!

'That's settled then,' said Miss Sprottle. 'Tomorrow we'll collect Master Bone from the gatehouse, where he will be, I know, most comfortable with Mr and Mrs Peters, and then we'll get on our way. I'm very eager to introduce you to Mr Entwhistle and enlist your help in solving our, I mean, his, I mean, the Museum's terrible, *terrible* dilemma . . . Oh, I do beg your pardon!' Here she paused to retrieve a hairpin from Slightly's now empty plate.

Slightly noticed how Miss Sprottle's face had gone all pink and pleased at the mention of Mr Entwhistle while *at the same time* she was looking serious and appalled about the vandalism. For a moment it was an interesting battle and then . . .

'We look forward to meeting Mr Entwhistle,' said Granny kindly, and the pink and pleased won the day!

'I – we – I mean – you must be tired!' Miss Sprottle stammered. 'Let me show you to your bedrooms – I hope you don't mind – they're nothing grand – just the study bedrooms the students use in term time.'

Nobody did mind. The rooms were plain but homely, and the narrow beds with their white coverlets were remarkably inviting after the long day.

Slightly snuggled down, her head full of wild students and bicycles and mummies and cursed necklaces. *I can't wait for it to be tomorrow – then I can really start solving this mystery!* She was smiling sleepily to herself when, all at once, she thought she heard a sound, coming from the grounds outside. It was an odd, squeaking noise ...

Tree branches blowing against each other in the wind, she thought with a yawn. *That'll be what it is. They make strange noises in the night.*

Slightly was fast asleep before she had a chance to notice that, just then, there was no wind.

✿

A little later, Mr Peters went out to walk round the college grounds and check that everything was as it should be.

He came to the bicycle shed.

'That's odd,' he said to himself. 'Miss Sprottle's Peggy's not here! She must have left it at the station after all. These intellectual ladies – forget their own heads if they weren't tied on!'

And with that, he put the matter out of his mind and went off to his bed.

Chapter Four:
Shattered

'There it is!' said Miss Sprottle proudly the next morning, as they climbed out of the cab. 'The Fitzwilliam Museum!'

Slightly stared in amazement at the building. Tall white columns soared up like stone palm trees and at the top carved figures in robes looked out over the rooftops. It reminded her of a picture of a Greek temple that Mr Westerly had shown her once, but plonked down in the middle of an English town.

What a splendid place for a mystery!

'And there's Mr Entwhistle!' Miss Sprottle added, even more proudly!

'Ah,' said Granny. 'Your young man.'

As Mr Entwhistle came down the steps to greet them he seemed to Slightly to be almost as extraordinary a sight as the Museum! At first glance, he reminded her of a human heron. He was very thin and his shoulders were stooped, maybe in a vain attempt to disguise his height, for he was exceptionally tall – a good head taller than most normal-sized men – and he *towered* over Miss Sprottle. He had a thin beaky nose and his eyes were beady and eager – as if he saw minnows swimming wherever he looked! *Could he be the criminal?* And then he looked at Slightly and smiled, and she could no more believe that he was a villain than she could fly.

'You must be Miss Jones,' he said to her. 'You know, it's impossible to see the carvings up on the front of the Museum properly from here. I always say the only people who have a decent view are the ones who own the chemist shop across the road.'

Slightly turned and looked speculatively at the shop while Miss Sprottle made the introductions. *I must question the chemist,* she thought to herself, though she guessed it was likely to be a dead end since the shop would be shut at night, when the crimes were committed. Then her attention jerked back to Mr Entwhistle.

'My dear Mellifluous will have told you of the terrible, terrible vandalism that is plaguing us here,' he was saying.

Ah-ha! thought Slightly.

'It really is like a curse – and as you know, it began not long after the arrival of what has come to be known as the Mummy's Necklace. Of course there is no connection between this lovely artefact and the lurid imaginings of my staff. Really, I'm as fond as the next man of a Penny Dreadful at the end of a day's work, but that's not to say I *believe* what I read there.'

Matthew snickered and Slightly didn't dare look at Granny for fear of bursting out giggling.

'And, er, do the police have no leads?' she asked quickly.

'None, Miss Jones. It's outrageous – they're not even taking it very seriously. Oh, I'm not suggesting they think there's a real mummy loose at the Museum. But they're not really as troubled by vandalism as they would be by actual theft. Apparently if the objects had been *stolen*, that would have been of much more interest to them. I almost wish they *had* been stolen. At least then they would still exist. It's the destruction that breaks my heart.'

Miss Forth sneezed suddenly, and at once he was all contrition.

'I'm so sorry – look at me, going on about my troubles and keeping you all standing in the cold – come in, do, please. I think you'll be impressed by our entrance hall . . .'

He was right! Inside, the whiteness of the exterior was forgotten. Everywhere Slightly looked she saw pink and black and gold and green. Two grand staircases of coloured marble swept up either side of the hall. More classical statues filled every niche and held up the door frames. The floor was covered with elaborately patterned mosaic, and the dome high above them and the painted glass windows would have graced a great cathedral.

Slightly's mouth dropped open.

'Oi! Don't you know it's rude to stare?' Matthew's voice in her ear made her jump. 'I thought *everybody* knew *that*!'

She turned on him crossly and was just about to give him a piece of her mind when she noticed an unhappy-looking man in a guard's uniform hovering to one side. He had *something's happened* written all over his face and was trying to get Mr Entwhistle's attention.

Miss Sprottle had seen him too. She gave her

fiancé a gentle tap on the arm. 'Er, Edward? I think . . .'

'What? Oh, yes, of course. If you'll excuse me? Mellifluous, my dear, perhaps you could tell our guests a little about the marble statues? You know more than any guide in the place.'

Miss Sprottle blushed, and everyone politely followed her over to the first of a number of classical statues – everyone, that is, except Slightly. She slid her notebook out of her pocket and slid herself behind a marble pillar. If something had happened, she wanted to know what it was!

'Going off duty now, are you, Rogers? Everything all right, I hope?' Mr Entwhistle spoke softly, leaning forward with an anxious smile.

The man shuffled his feet awkwardly. 'I don't like to say, Mr Entwhistle, sir,' he rumbled. 'He's a good man, Derek is, and I don't want to get him in any trouble.'

Mr Entwhistle's smile died and Slightly unscrewed her propelling pencil.

'What kind of trouble would that be, then?' he asked wearily. 'As if I didn't know.'

''Fraid so, sir. It's *her*. She's been seen again. Derek swears blind – begging your pardon, sir – he insists he saw the mummy, clear as anything.'

How exactly can you tell whether a mummy is a lady or a gentleman? wondered Slightly, but the guard was still speaking.

'She was there one minute, all silent and green and glowing and ghastly, and then, suddenly, the next minute, she was gone. Disappeared.'

'And, let me guess,' said Mr Entwhistle. 'No one else was with him? No one else saw or heard this impossibility? No strange wailing? No creaking doors?'

The guard shook his head unhappily.

'And have you doubled the number of night watchmen, as I asked?'

'I've tried, sir, I really have, but the men won't take the job, not while they think there's this here undead lady on the loose. Not even for double wages.'

'You'd have thought, with Christmas so close, they'd be grateful for a little extra,' Mr Entwhistle muttered bitterly.

'Well, sir, what they've been saying amongst themselves is that it's not much of a Christmas present to the family, sir, if you come home from work dead. Or undead, as the case may be. Sir.'

The guard stared down at the floor, then up at the ceiling. Then he coughed and inspected his boots. Slightly could clearly see from her hiding place that he had more to say, and that he was none too eager to say it.

'Out with it, man!' said Mr Entwhistle. 'Let me know the worst!'

The guard looked as if he were about to cry.

'The fourth-century glass bowl, sir. Shattered ... beyond repair ... The photographer has just been to record the remains – I know how careful you are, sir ...' But he was talking to thin air. Mr Entwhistle had already rushed away.

Miss Sprottle, seeing him go, murmured, 'Oh, no!' and hurried after him – and Miss Forth, Granny and Matthew hurried after *her*. For a moment Slightly hesitated, torn between her desire to see the scene of the crime without delay and her desire to question the guard . . . But when the man blew his nose vigorously and stomped away, muttering about finding himself a nice strong cup of tea before anything *else* went wrong, Slightly realised that he was probably not in the best mood for conversation.

She caught up with the others in the Egyptian Room. They were clustered around a sad little pile of jagged, broken glass in an exhibition case. Beside it was a notice that read 'Egyptian Glass Bowl'. Otherwise it would have been impossible to tell *what* had stood there. It was as if someone had taken a hammer to it.

A hammer, thought Slightly. She chewed on her propelling pencil for a moment. There was something that didn't add up here, but she just couldn't put her finger on it.

'Such a beautiful piece – so delicate, so fragile – so *miraculous* to have survived while empires come and go and mountains crumble and seas disappear ... And that this should happen while it was in *my* care – oh, who would do such a thing?' Mr Entwhistle was murmuring sadly, and everyone else was tutting in sympathy and trying to comfort him.

Wait a minute!

Slightly tried to interrupt as politely as she could manage. 'Please – could I ask – was nothing *heard*? Surely even a dead person can't smash a glass bowl without there being any *sound* ...'

She trailed off, realising no one was paying any attention to her. Someone else had come into the room.

'Wicked ... wicked ...' said a velvety voice.

'Oh,' said Mr Entwhistle. 'Gertrude – I mean, Miss Ponsonby.'

Matthew gave a low whistle. 'Blimey – what a bobby dazzler,' he whispered in Slightly's ear.

Slightly turned, and stared.

She had never seen anyone look less like a Gertrude in her whole life. Miss Ponsonby was, as Matthew had said, dazzling. She was willowy and graceful and her dark skin put the pale faces around her to shame, and her black hair shone like the coat of a panther. But all that was eclipsed by the beauty of her eyes. They were the eyes of an Egyptian goddess.

She was holding a small pan and brush.

'Ah, Miss Ponsonby! I wish I could have spared you this . . . this sacrilege!' said Mr Entwhistle. '*Another* of these senseless attacks . . .' He choked up, and could only shake his head in bewilderment.

Miss Ponsonby smiled a small, soulful smile, looking even more utterly beautiful as she did so. Slightly noticed Miss Sprottle shifting a little closer to her fiancé.

'It is only right that I am the one to deal with the remains,' Miss Ponsonby spoke as if the shards of glass had been something once living. 'Though it is apparent that nothing can be saved here, it is still my duty and my responsibility to do my best to try. As I have tried, and failed, so many times before.' She looked sideways at Miss Sprottle and her guests. 'I am the Museum's humble conservator, in the time I can spare from my studies at Girton College.'

Miss Sprottle jumped. 'Oh, forgive me – allow me to introduce my friends. They too are most concerned by these terrible acts.'

'Yes,' said Slightly, stepping forward eagerly. 'In fact, there are a number of questions I'd very much like to ask you . . .'

Miss Ponsonby looked down at her, and smiled with her lovely mouth, but not with her lovely eyes. 'Sweet,' she murmured. 'What a charming little girl.' And then, to Slightly's surprise, she patted her on the head like a puppy and turned away.

'Er, no, I meant I would like to interview you, about the crimes, you know?' *Maybe she didn't understand me*, thought Slightly, holding up her notebook as a kind of explanation.

Miss Ponsonby didn't seem to hear or see her. She stepped up to Mr Entwhistle and murmured, 'Perhaps it is time to inform our superiors . . . ?'

'Eh? Oh.' Mr Entwhistle sighed and nodded. 'Yes, you're right. I must go and make my report of this latest outrage to the head of the Museum.' And to Granny and the others he added, 'Please, do not let this terrible business spoil your visit – this room of course will be closed for the moment . . .' He trailed off, staring sadly down at the shattered glass. 'What was I saying? Yes, the rest of the Museum –

we have many fine exhibits. I . . . I leave you in Mellifluous's capable hands . . .' He straightened his shoulders as far as they would go and trudged away.

Miss Ponsonby, meanwhile, stepped forward with her little pan and brush. With graceful gestures, she began to sweep up the shards. But several of the pieces had become jammed into the side of the display case. She set the brush aside and tried to get one out with her fingers . . .

'Careful – you'll hurt yourself!' warned Granny. But it was too late. Slightly saw the line of blood blossom across the side of her hand and begin to trickle down her wrist.

Granny reached over. 'There now, you don't want to get blood on your white blouse . . .' she said, pushing Miss Ponsonby's sleeve up to keep it clear of the wound.

'You're very kind – please don't bother – the blouse is old –' Miss Ponsonby detached herself from Granny abruptly, pulling her sleeve down again.

But not before Slightly saw something that made her draw in her breath in shock.

Miss Ponsonby's arm was covered in bruises. And to Slightly's horror, they looked exactly as if they'd been made by someone's fingers.

Chapter Five:
Catch Me, Gertrude!

It was a subdued group that gathered for lunch in a quiet back room of a nearby coach house. They'd done their best to appreciate the lovely things on display in the many rooms of the Fitzwilliam Museum, but it was hard to forget the sad little pile of broken glass. Slightly had spent the whole time thinking about the whys and hows and whos and what ifs. Her brain was struggling to make a clear, sensible picture of the crime, but images of a glowing green mummy silently passing its dead hands over the vase and magically reducing it to rubble kept pushing their way to the front.

Even Miss Sprottle's cheerfulness was strained.

'If only I could really help him, but what can I do?' Slightly heard her saying in a low voice to Granny. 'I'm just a linguist. I can put words together. Miss Ponsonby's skills as a restorer, on the other hand ...'

'Are admirable, no doubt,' Granny finished for her, 'but I'm sure Mr Entwhistle would much rather not have to make use of them!'

Miss Sprottle sighed and shook her head. Slightly looked down at her plate. Miss Ponsonby was a troubling character, and no mistake. Had she imagined the marks on her arms? Nobody else had mentioned them. And why wouldn't she answer her questions? Of course lots of people didn't take girl detectives seriously. If everybody who treated her like a child automatically became a suspect, she'd need a much bigger notebook!

But then Miss Sprottle made her forget all about that.

She pulled a folder out of her handbag. 'You may not realise, but we have a photographic record of each incident, before and after pictures. I brought them to show you all –' But then she paused uncertainly. 'Though it's rude of me to interrupt your lunch . . .' And she made as if to put the folder away again.

'Please pass the salt,' muttered Matthew, who was paying closer attention to his food than to the conversation.

Call yourself a detective? HA! thought Slightly, laying her notebook open on the table beside her plate. Even though her own mouth was full of cold beef at the time she turned to Miss Sprottle and said, a little indistinctly, 'Please! We'd love to see – after all, evidence is the best sauce!'

Miss Sprottle smiled. 'Ah! Is that one of Mr Sherlock Holmes's clever sayings?'

Slightly swallowed and picked up her pencil. 'No – just one of Miss Slightly Jones's clever sayings!'

Matthew started to make a rude noise, then quickly turned it into a mimsy little cough.

Granny gave him a warning look. 'Yes, do show us what you've brought, if you'd be so kind.'

Miss Sprottle drew a sheaf of photographs from the folder. 'Edward is very modern, you know. He insists on a photographic record of every artefact in his department – indeed, if he had his way, every item in the Museum would be photographed as part of their cataloguing. That's the way of the future, he says.' And she laid the photos carefully out on the tablecloth. 'These are the pieces as they came to us . . .'

And there they were − the funeral statues, the clay jars, Egyptian animals, enigmatic hieroglyphs on scraps of papyrus − each artefact proudly photographed − the best of modern technology brought to the service of the best of ancient art.

'These little statues were placed in the tomb with the pharaohs and their queens to serve them in the afterlife − see how carefully they have been painted to look as real as possible? And here, on this papyrus, aren't the hieroglyphs intriguing? We are learning more all the time about how to read their secrets. This hippo statue is thought to be the goddess Taweret. And these are canopic jars, which held the bits of the body that were taken out during mummification . . . though that is not perhaps the most appropriate lunchtime topic . . .'

Slightly was about to disagree − she wanted to know *which* bits went into the jars − but Granny intervened.

'Tell us about *this* picture, Miss Sprottle,' she said firmly, pointing at the photograph of a small statue of what looked like a dog with a very long tail.

'Ah, yes − I think this was my favourite,' said Miss Sprottle sadly. 'This is Anubis in his jackal form.

He was the god of mummification and the afterlife and we see him in many different shapes – but here he sits with his paws peacefully out in front and that endearingly long tail hanging down behind. So appealing!'

Miss Sprottle sighed and laid out the rest of the photos. 'And these are the records of what became of each . . .'

The shattered remains. Anonymous piles of broken glass and crumbled papyrus and smashed plaster, wood and clay. And in the background of every one of this second set of photographs, there was Miss Ponsonby, looking lovely and sad and noble, and holding her little pan and brush.

Slightly felt a wave of angry determination flood over her. *This has got to STOP! I must find the answer – I must solve this case!*

But determination wasn't enough. *Method, Slightly,* she reminded herself. *Careful sifting – leave no stone unturned.* 'Do you think there's anything you haven't mentioned to us yet, Miss Sprottle? Anything at all?'

Miss Sprottle shook her head. 'I told Sally everything in my letter!'

'Perhaps we should go over it again, just to be sure? No detail must be left out, no matter how small or inconsequential it might seem.'

Sadly, however, Miss Sprottle really did have nothing new to add. By the time they'd gone over the story again the lunch hour was well and truly over. And Slightly had to admit that they were no further forward on the why or the how.

'So perhaps we should have a look at the *who*. Suspects, any and all, possible and impossible. We should start alphabetically. Now, who do we know who has anything at all to do with this case, whose name begins with A?'

'Professor Amberleigh?' said Miss Forth.

At which Miss Sprottle startled them all by jumping up, hairpins flying, and crying out, 'GOOD HEAVENS!'

'What's the matter, Miss Sprottle!' exclaimed Granny.

'Miss Amberleigh's public lecture! It will have begun!'

'OH!'

They rushed back to the Museum as fast as they could, but they were still late.

'The tour's already started, ma'am,' said the young man at the door. 'But you can catch it up in the Egyptian rooms if you hurry.'

They thanked him and dashed off.

'Along here,' whispered Miss Sprottle. 'I can hear

Miss Amberleigh's voice.' They turned into the exhibition room, attached themselves to the back of the crowd and tried to pretend they'd been there all along.

'Look – there's Miss Ponsonby,' whispered Matthew. She was at the edge of the group as well, standing with an unprepossessing young man with floppy hair and no chin.

'That's Freddy Twist,' Miss Sprottle whispered. 'He's one of the assistants here at the Museum. Edward tells me he's always following Miss Ponsonby around. Utterly besotted, Edward says.'

'Amazing they get anything done around here, all the lovey-dovey that's going on,' muttered Matthew.

Slightly shushed him, smothering a grin.

'I can't see the professor from back here,' she whispered, craning her neck without success. 'Everybody's too tall!'

But Professor Amberleigh was on the move, and Slightly got her first clear view of the owner of the resounding voice.

She was an impressive sight – a large woman in height and breadth, she seemed to take up twice as much space as anyone else. She walked majestically, with the straight, unbending posture of someone who is severely corseted.

She certainly looks strong enough to have made those marks on Miss Ponsonby's arm, thought Slightly with a shiver.

'I will take you now to the next room,' the professor announced loudly. 'You may ask me any questions as we proceed . . .'

The crowd parted respectfully, pushing Slightly and the others back against the wall as the professor passed. A dapper little man was scuttling along beside her. He clearly had a question to ask.

'Tell me, madam —'

'I prefer to be addressed as Professor.'

'Oh, yes, indeed, er, Madam Professor, what would you say to those who question Britain's right to excavate in other countries? Excavate and then remove what they find?'

Slightly was surprised. She'd never thought of that before.

But Professor Amberleigh knew exactly what *she* thought.

'I'd say they're fools,' she boomed. 'Look around you. This fine building, these grand rooms — fitting settings for the glories of the past. And none more glorious than the past of Egypt. For thousands of years she was without doubt the greatest civilization the world has ever produced. But that is long gone.

Modern Egypt is now nothing but a dirty country squatting in the shadows of a distant heyday. The people are little better than savages and can't be expected to look after such treasures.'

Slightly noticed that all around her people were nodding agreement. Only a few shuffled their feet and looked uncomfortable.

Mr Twist, however, turned beetroot.

'Professor!' he gasped. 'Oh, no, really, I say!' Slightly could see his Adam's apple bobbing up and down alarmingly.

'What?'

He lowered his voice. 'Aren't you forgetting . . . I mean to say . . . you're forgetting that Miss Ponsonby is Egyptian.'

'What? Oh, that. She's only *half* Egyptian. Her father was English.'

The matter settled, Professor Amberleigh strode on towards the next cluster of exhibition cases. Mr Twist seemed not to know what to do or where to look. Miss Ponsonby, however, kept her eyes modestly down and followed on with a quiet grace.

'What a rude woman!' Granny tutted disapprovingly as they trailed after the crowd, and Slightly agreed.

'And now we come to the centrepiece of the

museum's Egyptian collection.' There was a new note in Professor Amberleigh's voice, a suppressed excitement that Slightly hadn't heard before. She peered and craned, trying in vain to get a clear view through the spectators as the professor continued, 'It has been described as the jewel in the Fitzwilliam's crown, but in my opinion it is far more beautiful than *any* crown. I am speaking, of course, of what is being called in the vulgar press "the Mummy's Necklace".'

There was a chorus of 'Oooh!'s from the crowd and everyone edged a step closer.

'Stop fidgeting!' whispered Granny.

'I can't see!' Slightly hissed back. Even on tiptoe she could only catch tantalising glimpses of the top of the professor's head. 'I want to see the cursed necklace!'

'Shh!' said Granny. 'It isn't cursed!' but Slightly wasn't there to hear. She was already squirming forward through the crowd wherever she could find – or make – a gap.

'Matthew, go with her,' said Granny. But Matthew was already on his way.

They made it through to the front of the crowd just as the professor started speaking again.

'There has been a great deal of outrageous

rumour and superstitious nonsense bandied about regarding this artefact and the so-called "Cambridge Mummy". I intend to dispel that stupidity once and for all. It is not usual Museum practice to handle the exhibits more than is absolutely necessary, but today I mean to make an exception. My assistant, Miss Ponsonby, will place the Mummy's Necklace around my neck so that you may see its beauty more closely – and also so that you can all see just how very *un*cursed it is!'

The crowd chuckled dutifully, though someone at the back muttered, 'Rather you than me, madam!'

Miss Ponsonby drew closer and whispered in Miss Amberleigh's ear. She seemed to be trying to dissuade her from her experiment, but the older woman waved her off abruptly.

'Gertrude! The necklace!'

Miss Ponsonby opened the case and took out the necklace, fumbling a little with the clasp.

'Careful!' barked the professor.

'I'm sorry, Professor,' Miss Ponsonby murmured.

Everyone leaned forward as the Mummy's Necklace was settled across Miss Amberleigh's bosom. For a moment she stood perfectly still, in a majestic pose. Then she began to stalk forward, gliding, almost.

'See how excellent the workmanship is. This is truly a gift worthy of a queen. Only a queen . . . only a . . .'

The words died with a gurgle. Miss Amberleigh staggered suddenly, clutched her throat with one hand and pointed, shaking visibly, with the other.

What a performance, thought Slightly in disgust. *Talk about over-acting!*

Which was when she noticed that the trembling finger was pointing straight at herself!

With a gasp, the crowd drew back and Slightly was left standing on her own. The professor's face was appalling – the blood had drained from it, and the whites of her eyes were showing all the way around, like a frightened horse.

'See! See there!' she cried. Slightly looked frantically about, but there was no escape. The professor was definitely pointing at *her*. 'It's a little Celtic slave-girl! She has come to serve me, out of the scented past. The mist . . . the mist is rising . . . I . . . I . . . Catch me, Gertrude!'

No one did catch her, however, and Miss Amberleigh collapsed onto the floor with a resounding thud.

Everyone began to jabber at once.

'What's happened?'

'She's fainted!

'No – it's the curse – she's dead!'

'It was that girl – she *did* something to her!'

'I didn't!' squeaked Slightly. 'I didn't do anything!'

'Who *is* she? Is she *the mummy*?!'

'The professor recognised her and then –'

The noise level rose. Meanwhile Miss Ponsonby was hovering over the prone professor, ineffectively trying to wave the crowd away.

'Step back, if you please – give her air . . .'

No one was paying her any attention. The crowd was fast becoming hysterical when, to Slightly's great relief, Miss Sprottle pushed her way to the front and took charge.

'Stop that this instant!' she scolded. 'Of course the professor has fainted – the heat in here is ridiculous, especially with everyone crowding her – you there, get back – give the poor woman some air.' She glared fiercely around. 'I've said it before and I'll say it again – what you see here is yet another victim to the barbaric custom of wearing corsets!'

At the word *corsets* all the ladies looked shocked and covered their children's ears and all the gentlemen tried to look as if they didn't know what it meant! But it did the trick. The crowd pulled back and broke up into tight little whispering groups.

Slightly's thoughts were leaping about in her head like scared rabbits.

What just happened? (Apart from Miss Sprottle mentioning corsets in public, which was shocking enough.)

Could she have seen what she thought she had?

I must be wrong. I must have misunderstood.

And yet she couldn't quite forget that brief expression of loathing she thought she'd seen, when Miss Amberleigh cried out, 'Catch me, Gertrude!' and her faithful assistant had carefully, deliberately, stepped *back* . . .

It didn't make sense – the professor's words didn't make sense – that pointing finger – everybody staring at her accusingly . . .

'Steady on, Slightly,' said Granny, suddenly at her shoulder. She raised her voice. 'I don't think we're needed here – I think the sooner everyone goes home, the better, don't you agree?'

At that moment, Mr Entwhistle rushed into the room. Mr Twist had gone for him. As soon it was made clear to him that Miss Sprottle, at least, was in no way harmed, he raised his voice, 'That's right, ladies and gentlemen. The tour is over. Miss, er, Professor Amberleigh is indisposed.' He caught sight of a guard gawking in the doorway and gestured him over. 'I need you to show the ladies and gentlemen out. Please, if you'll all just follow the guard, yes, thank you, good day, thank you, thank you . . .'

As the last straggler reluctantly left the room, Mr Entwhistle turned back, looking extremely harried.

'What was she playing at?' he muttered. 'We do not make exhibits of ourselves with the, er, exhibits! Mr Twist, you'd better run across the street to the chemist and purchase some smelling salts.'

'I fear it may be closed, sir,' said Mr Twist. 'The holidays, you know . . .'

'Then find a police constable! Police constables still carry smelling salts, don't they – or has our entire civilization gone completely mad?' Mr Twist scurried away and Mr Entwhistle regarded the problem on the floor in front of him.

'Now, Miss Ponsonby, if you would be so good as to remove that wretched necklace and return it to its proper place.'

'Yes, Mr Entwhistle,' said Miss Ponsonby. Slightly couldn't help noticing how gracefully she sank to the ground to do so.

'Ooooh . . . where am I?' moaned the professor.

Was it coincidence, or did Professor Amberleigh begin to revive the very the moment the mummy's necklace was removed? Slightly couldn't decide *what* was going on. Was Professor Amberleigh just a great big show-off, or had she somehow actually become possessed? Could it possibly be that *she* was the one destroying the Museum's treasures? Had the curse really lain dormant all those thousands of years until, now, it was unleashed in wintry Cambridge?

Slightly shivered – and then found she couldn't stop!

'Matthew, Sally, cup of tea,' said Granny firmly, and taking Slightly by the arm, she led the way out of the room, out of the Museum and onto Trumpington Street.

They passed Mr Twist charging up the front steps. His pale face was now scarlet from all his exertions and he clutched a small green-glass bottle of smelling salts in his hand, holding it as far away from himself as possible, as if it were something that was about to explode.

'Got it from the constable,' he panted. 'I was lucky – he was just going off shift for the holiday.' He plunged through the front doors.

'It'll take more 'n' smelling salts to bring that loonie to her senses,' grunted Matthew.

'That's not a very gentlemanly thing to say,' said Granny. 'But I think I quite agree.'

CHAPTER SIX:
In the Dark

Slightly moaned. She was trapped in a space so tight she could touch the walls on either side. There was a lid, too, that her fingers scrabbled against. And darkness that weighed down, stifling the breath in her throat. There was something unfamiliar around her neck. She tried to scream but no sound came.

She knew without knowing how that she was in a sarcophagus, buried deep under the ground, and that it would be thousands of years before anyone would find her — thousands and thousands of years – the thing round her neck was as heavy as hatred, as inescapable as a cobra – the curse – she could never escape the curse –

With a gasp, Slightly sat bolt upright in her bed.

She was safe in her room in Girton College. *It was just a dream . . . just a dream . . .* She untangled the blankets and lay down again, doing her best to still her ragged breathing.

It took a long time, but she was beginning at last to drift off when something snapped her awake again. She didn't know what – the call of a night bird, perhaps, or the distant slam of a door – but whatever it was, she was tempted to ignore it. She was worn out. She just wanted to get some sleep. *Though a real detective always investigates*, she told herself. *Day or night. Even when that detective's bed is warm and her room is cold . . .*

With a sigh, she got up and stumbled over to the window. Her eyes were blurry with sleep. The patterns of frost on the glass obscured the view. The moon was draped by wisps of cloud. And yet Slightly could have sworn she saw something down there. Something that shone strangely – something that glided over the ground without seeming to touch it, swooping and dancing, flickering in and out of sight – there and not there, and there again.

Greenly glowing, a spectre was dancing on the grass of Girton College.

The Cambridge Mummy . . .

Slightly rubbed her eyes. *This is impossible! What would the mummy be doing HERE?!* She scrubbed at the frosted window, trying to get a clearer view, but every time she got close enough to look out, her breath fogged the glass again. She fumbled with the latch and finally managed to drag the window open.

The cold air made her gasp but at last she could see . . .

. . . nothing. There was nothing to see. The lawn was empty and quiet.

Well, of course it is, Slightly scolded herself. *There's no such thing as walking mummies or dancing ones either.*

She closed the window with a bang and jumped into bed. *I'll be awake all night now!* she thought and then, suddenly, midway through a huge yawn, she was asleep again.

❦

'I declare today a holiday!' exclaimed Miss Sprottle next morning. 'It's Christmas Eve!'

Slightly frowned. *That's all very well,* she thought grumpily, *but will the vandal be taking a holiday?*

Would Sherlock Holmes take a holiday, if HE were in the middle of a case? Though, to be honest, she wasn't exactly in the middle of *anything*. She had no real evidence, no clear suspects (living ones, anyway), no discernible motives – nothing but embarrassing finger-pointing, bad dreams and midnight imaginings.

'Compliments of the season, dear ladies!'

It was Mr Entwhistle, his arms laden with ivy and holly, and close on his heels, Matthew and Mr Peters bringing in a lovely fir tree they'd fetched in the college cart. They were all three so bright and brisk that Slightly couldn't help but begin to feel better.

'Over there, I think – if you'd be so kind?'

They set up the tree with more enthusiasm than efficiency, but eventually it stood, on a tilt, in the corner of the library. Miss Forth and Granny took over the long table where the students worked on Latin and Greek and Mathematics in term time, and laid out coloured cardboard and a glue pot and scissors, ribbons and fabric and postcards and a paint box. Miss Sprottle and Mr Entwhistle were soon giggling and whispering as they made a mistletoe ball together. Matthew was set cutting and pasting paper chains. In an astonishingly short length of time he had glue on his hands, on his face, in his hair and, now and then, on the coloured strips.

'Here you go, Slightly,' said Granny. 'It's ivy ribbons for you!'

Even though sewing wasn't something she normally enjoyed, Slightly set to with good will. It was Christmas Eve, and nobody was going to be passing judgment on a few wonky stitches.

Miss Sprottle told stories about some of the pranks the Girton girls got up to (like sliding down a full flight of stairs on a tea tray – Slightly was instantly determined to give that a go!) and Miss Forth sang Christmas carols in her reedy high voice and Mr Entwhistle asked riddles, to uproarious laughter. They had a scratch lunch of cold mutton, bread and cheese, and the tree, still on a bit of a slant, grew more and more beautiful. The short winter day was already drawing to a close, when the door opened. Everyone looked up in surprise.

I'd forgotten there was anybody else here! thought Slightly, as Miss Ponsonby glided in.

'Do excuse me,' she murmured in her velvety voice. 'I was looking for a book . . .'

Slightly could tell she wasn't the only one who felt suddenly guilty. They'd all been having such a lovely time, and Miss Ponsonby had been working . . .

'Er, are you going to Evensong at King's College today, Miss Ponsonby?' asked Miss Sprottle.

'Oh, Miss Sprottle, you can't imagine how much I look forward to it! I wish to be there, oh, most certainly – I wouldn't miss those angelic voices for the world!' She clasped her hands together, looking utterly angelic herself. 'Illness prevented me last year – I had only just arrived from a warmer climate and had not yet grown to love England's mists and snow and long, long nights, as I do now. I will certainly see you there, though, as I am told there is always such a crowd, *you* might not see *me*.' And she looked down, so that her dark lashes lay on her cheek in a bewitching picture of maiden modesty.

Slightly tried to be objective, even though Miss Ponsonby had ignored her request for an interview. Even though she had patted her on the head. *It's not her fault she's so beautiful.* A little voice in her head added, *Just like you can't help looking like a ferret . . .*

'And will Professor Amberleigh be going? Though of course that will depend on her health,' said Granny a little sharply.

'Ah. You are referring to the incident in the Museum, with the little girl.' Miss Ponsonby nodded. 'I do hope no upset was caused. After her little episodes, the professor rarely remembers anything she may have done. Otherwise, I am sure she would have made an effort to apologise to you all in person.'

Slightly caught Matthew's eye. *Told you — loonie,* he mouthed at her, nodding smugly.

'Do you think she will be well enough to attend Evensong?' asked Miss Sprottle.

'It is not certain. I feel sure that an evening of sublime music would do her so much good, but of course she is the best judge . . . Though I do long to go.' The last words were barely more than a sigh.

She collected the book and glided away. But the happy spell seemed to have been broken. Before long, Miss Sprottle and Mr Entwhistle were having a whispered quarrel, Miss Forth was scolding Matthew for making a mess, Granny's mouth had gone as tight as a letter box — and Slightly was in disgrace. She'd jabbed her finger with the needle as she sewed what felt like her four-hundredth ivy leaf, lost her temper and used one of Matthew's more colourful expressions.

'Perhaps a little exercise is called for?' suggested Miss Forth. 'There is still some time before we will be leaving for Evensong.'

'This place would be perfect for Hide and Go Seek,' said Matthew. 'I'm a demon at Hide and Go Seek.'

Slightly's chin went up. 'Says you. I could give you a two-day head start and I'd still be able to find you.'

'Anything – just stay out of here till we can get everything tidied up!' Granny was looking harassed.

'And of course you must also stay out of the students' rooms,' added Miss Sprottle.

'Of course,' said Slightly.

'And the chapel, and the laboratory, and don't go outside unless you put on your coat and hat and gloves and for goodness' sake don't hide *in* anything where you could get trapped . . .'

Matthew had already ducked out of the door. Slightly started counting furiously. She'd show him!

'– ninety-nine, a hundred – ready or not, here I come!'

Slightly threw herself into the passageway. As she hesitated for a second – Should I go left? Or right? – the library door swung shut behind her. For a moment she could see nothing but darkness, but then her eyes adjusted. Stretching away in both directions, the corridor with its Gothic arches was only dimly visible, the widely spaced gas lights giving little away.

What was that? A door slammed somewhere in the depth of the building – Slightly gritted her teeth and was off.

'Come out, come out, wherever you are,' she whispered as she ran. *Unless you're a mummy!* she added silently.

The college was so big and empty and echoey and strange that Slightly found herself hoping that Matthew really *wasn't* extra good at Hide and Go Seek! She kept going, but she was running on tiptoe now, her breath coming faster and faster . . .

And then she heard something that made the hairs on the back of her neck stand up.

Someone, somewhere in the big empty building, was singing. It was a strange, wordless, wailing song, infinitely sad. Infinitely exotic.

Trying not to breathe, Slightly crept forward. She came to the foot of a staircase. The steps were in shadow. And there was Matthew, standing dead still, listening. She was sure she hadn't made a sound, but he turned towards her anyway, and put his finger to his lips.

The singing was coming from somewhere overhead. It made Slightly think of places far away, places ruled by heat and dust. The music was muted at first and then grew louder, as if the singer had turned towards them, as if she were singing now *to* them, drawing them into her web of sound. The cold of the stone floor working its way through Slightly's shoes – the low fizzing of the gas lamps in the corridor behind her – the darkness of a winter afternoon at the window – they all faded, and only this song of the south seemed real. A faint, strange scent hung in the air for a moment, and then was gone. Without realising what she was doing, Slightly took a step forward. And another. And another. Her foot knocked against the bottom step – and the singing stopped abruptly.

'Look,' breathed Matthew.

A disembodied face floated in the dimness above them, looking down.

The mummy!

She hadn't realised she'd clutched Matthew's arm until she heard him squeak in protest.

And then the face spoke. 'Who's there?'

Slightly let out her breath in a whoosh.

'Miss Ponsonby?' said Matthew. There was a distinct quaver in his voice. 'Is that you? Blimey, you didn't half scare me! I mean, us.'

Miss Ponsonby came down the stairs towards them. 'What are you doing here?' she said. Her velvety voice was a little huskier than usual. 'You shouldn't be wandering about the college like this – it's not a playground for little children. Are you pretending to be a real-life detective again? Is that the game you are playing?'

Slightly gritted her teeth. How dare Miss Ponsonby treat her like a silly child! What made it worse was the knowledge that they *had* been using the college as a playground! She spoke up determinedly, 'Well, as you mention it, Miss Ponsonby, there *are* some questions I would very much like to ask . . .'

'Gertrude? Gertrude!' A querulous voice echoed from above. 'Where are you?'

And at the same moment, from along the corridor . . .

'Slightly! Matthew!' Someone was calling them.

'You are wanted also,' said Miss Ponsonby, turning on the stairs and starting back up again. 'Be so good as to tell Miss Sprottle and the others that I will not be at Evensong. The professor needs me.'

'Come on,' Matthew muttered. 'I've had enough running around in the dark for one day!' He stalked off down the corridor.

But Slightly stood frozen to the spot. She was staring at the place where Miss Ponsonby had been standing. She couldn't believe her eyes.

There, on the wall, was a luminous handprint. For a moment it glowed in the dim light, green and otherworldly, and then it faded away.

CHAPTER SEVEN:
Mist and Mystery

'The cab will be here any minute,' said Granny. 'Quickly now, both of you, put on your coats. Come on.'

Slightly's thoughts were full of mummies and glowing handprints and vandalism and curses. She barely noticed as Granny bundled her up and hurried her towards the door. She stepped out, stopped still, and gasped.

'Blimey!' said Matthew. Slightly waved her hand about in front of her face.

It wasn't as if she'd never seen fog before. Growing up in London, she'd coughed and hacked her way through Peasoupers and London Particulars so thick and greasy and greeny-grey that you could get lost a few yards from your front door. Made up of polluted air and fumes and unspeakable mists rising up out of the dirty Thames, they crept along the cobbled streets and back alleys like an evil invasion. This fog was *nothing* like that.

For one thing, it was *white*, and it drifted like fine muslin over pale velvet snow. The moon was full, but looked three times its normal size because of the misty circles of light around it. As they stood staring, amazed, the cab arrived. The horse appeared to be swimming its way though silvery whiteness that parted in swathes to let it pass.

Slightly couldn't find any words, but she smiled at Granny. *Maybe Miss Sprottle is right. It's Christmas Eve. Maybe it's time to take a break from ugliness and destruction and curses . . .*

As they climbed into the cab and began the trip into the town, everyone was silent, mesmerised by the view on either side. The mist swirled up sometimes till it covered the cab windows, then sometimes it dropped away so that they could see trees rising up blackly at the roadside, their tops coppiced into fingers that reached for the sky.

As the horse clip-clopped down Magdalene Street and over the bridge, Slightly looked down into a river of filmy mist that stretched away between the buildings. Half-seen, the colleges were like fairytale castles, ancient and mysterious. Gaslight and candlelight shone yellow-gold out of windows and hung in the air around the street lamps.

Beautiful, thought Slightly. *Beautiful.*

The streets were crowded now, with carriages and cabs and people walking, all headed towards the chapel. Along the narrow, cobbled ways they came – along Petty Cury and Peas Hill, Burrell's Walk and Trinity Lane, Silver Street and Green Street and Botolph Passage, all leading at last into King's Parade.

'Let us out, driver,' said Miss Sprottle. 'We'll walk the rest of the way.'

As they climbed down from the cab and joined the crowd, Slightly looked into the faces around her. Everywhere she saw the same. Friends greeted each other with subdued smiles and even the babies, carried over shoulders and staring wide-eyed and solemn, were quiet.

They walked on until they came out into the place where the street widened, and there it was – King's College Chapel, rising out of the mist like a tall ship, lit from within. Slightly stopped to stare.

'Hurry up, Slightly,' Granny called. 'We don't want to get separated.'

They already were. The throng was moving on – Slightly could see Granny trying to come back for her, but the crowd was too dense, and too determined. Slightly waved encouragingly and called out, 'I'm fine – don't worry!' But a large gentleman frowned and shushed her, saying, 'You're entering a *church*, young lady!'

She could hear the organ music, drifting out into the night. She could see the flickering light of hundreds of candles through the open doorway, and a glimpse of the white carved walls, the stained-glass windows darkened by the darkness outside. She could imagine the fluted ceiling, like stone palm trees high over head.

It's going to be wonderful, she thought. *Magical.*

'Excuse me, please, if you'd let me pass,' a panic-stricken voice spoke at her elbow. She looked down into the red and anxious face of a very small choirboy.

'Hello!' she said, but the boy just shook his head, as if Hellos were of no use to him. 'What's wrong?'

'I'm late, miss, awful late, and the choirmaster's going to *kill* me!' He was close to tears.

'Where do you need to get to?' she asked him.

'Round the back, miss. We're meant to line up

there, ready to process in, but the crowds got in the way and no one will let me past . . .'

Slightly bent down and gave him a friendly grin. 'Follow me . . .'

And she ducked down and began to weasel her way sideways through the crowd, the tiny choirboy in tow. Their path was erratic, marked by startled squeals and jumps, but determination and a sharp pair of elbows won the day, and soon the choirboy was lined up with his fellows, and having his cassock and collar tweaked and straightened by the choirmaster, who was too relieved at his arrival to even scold him properly.

Slightly waved goodbye to the boy and headed back to the main door of the chapel with a satisfied smile. She attached herself to the back of the crowd and waited patiently to enter.

'Wind's up,' someone said, and there was a murmur of agreement.

Slightly turned round and saw that the mist was indeed beginning to disperse. In the sky, the big round moon suddenly blazed with cold light.

How remarkable, she thought, *that hundreds of miles away, people will be looking at just the same moon as me.* She imagined a girl gazing out of a window in Moscow, or a sailor out on the heaving Atlantic, or someone somewhere hot and ancient and full of mysteries. Somewhere like Egypt . . .

Which is when she saw them. Miss Ponsonby and Professor Amberleigh, muffled yet unmistakeable, in the college cart, driving along King's Parade, keeping as far into the shadows as the horse could go.

And stranger still, sticking up out of the cart, was Miss Sprottle's bicycle!

CHAPTER EIGHT:
Ladies First

Every thought of Christmas Eve and Evensong fled from Slightly's head. She was a detective again, through and through! *Suspicious behaviour calls for immediate investigation*, she told herself, and started to run.

The last of the mist had vanished, and she felt the cold begin to bite under the clear sky. She shivered, but it wasn't only the wintry chill. Behind them, in the chapel, she knew Granny would be worried at first. But then she'd think Slightly had found a seat further back —

not unreasonable in such a crowd. And ahead . . .
A wild goose chase? Or something else?

She shivered again and hugged the shadows.

The cart rumbled on along King's Parade and into
Trumpington Street. The horse slithered from time
to time on the icy cobbles and Slightly could hear
it whicker nervously.

Don't get too close. Don't let them see you. The great
white bulk of the Fitzwilliam Museum loomed
ahead. She was concentrating so hard on her quarry
it didn't occur to her that someone else might be
following *her*, until she was shoved abruptly into a
doorway and a hand was clamped over her mouth.
She struck out wildly . . .

''Ere – stow that!' whispered Matthew. 'It's me –
it's me!'

Slightly pulled away indignantly. 'What do
you think you're doing?! You could have ruined
everything – can't you see I'm trailing that cart?!'

'Oh, is that what you call it?' Matthew shook
his head sadly. 'Lucky for you I saw you leave. How
anyone as scrawny as you can make so much noise
is a mystery and no mistake.' When Slightly took a
deep, angry breath to reply, he held up a warning
finger. 'They'll hear you!'

Slightly swallowed her words and looked

anxiously out of the shadows. But there was no sign that the muffled figures on the cart were aware of being observed. They might have been carved from the same stone as the Fitzwilliam statues. Even when someone came out from behind the pillars, they barely acknowledged him.

'That's that Twist geezer,' whispered Matthew and Slightly nodded.

Freddy was clearly nervous. He looked up and down the moonlit streets, his eyes passing over their hiding place several times. But the shadows concealed them. Satisfied at last, Mr Twist went to the horse's head and led it down a side alley towards the back of the Museum.

The moment they were out of sight, Slightly started forward, but Matthew didn't move.

'Where are you waiting for?' she whispered urgently. 'We need to follow them – see if we can find a way in – find out what those three are up to. Come on – while there's a chance there's a back door open . . .'

But Matthew shook his head. 'No need. We'll go in at the front.' And he scurried up the steps and past the big pillars.

Slightly caught up with him at the main entrance. 'You're going to try to break in the front door of a famous museum full of priceless objects?! Are you crazy?! Don't you know they're going to have the best, most secure locks ever invented? It'll take you *hours* to crack them, unless you plan on just blowing them up, and don't you think that might just be a little noisy . . .'

With a quiet click, the front door of the Fitzwilliam Museum swung open.

There was a brief pause. Then . . .

'That's *amazing*!' gasped Slightly, impressed in spite of herself.

Matthew gave her a crooked grin. 'Oh well, not *so* amazing. When I saw you peel off like that after the bobby dazzler and the loonie, I half-inched Mr Entwhistle's keys.' He skipped back nimbly as Slightly tried to punch him and gave her a bow. 'Ladies first.'

The grand hallway looked strange by moonlight, all its colours muted into grey. Slightly waited as Matthew carefully relocked the door and pocketed the keys. She knew they wanted to head for the back of the Museum. She tried to remember the layout of the rooms, to decide the best route. But before she had a chance, something decided it for them.

The sound of footsteps coming from the lower

galleries. The kind of footsteps that heavy boots make.

'It's a guard!' hissed Matthew. 'Scarper!'

They fled up the stairs and into the first gallery they came to – but it would seem that their luck was out. The footsteps followed, loud and insistent.

'Hide!' hissed Matthew. He shoved Slightly behind a suit of armour and rolled under a cabinet himself just as the guard appeared.

Did he see us? Slightly held her breath. The guard was holding his lantern in front of him like a shield, and without pausing to look left or right, he practically ran along the long room. In fact, it was likely he wouldn't have noticed them if they'd made no move to hide at all. This was a man who didn't *want* to see anything out of the ordinary!

'Not paid enough . . .' she heard him mutter as he scurried past. 'Not nearly enough . . .'

And then he was gone. With a sigh of relief, she started to step out from behind the armour but Matthew waved her back abruptly.

Stay put! he mouthed, pointing to the spot with his finger as if he were the boss. Silent as a shadow, he was off, following the guard.

He's doing it again, Slightly thought indignantly. *Making out he's in charge and I'm just along for the ride!*

She was nobody's sidekick. On the other hand, it made sense to find out where the guard was going. And Matthew did have a lot more experience tailing people than she had. And it would be extremely embarrassing if the guard caught them . . . Hard to explain, really, what they were doing there . . .

Thoroughly disgruntled, Slightly stayed put.

It was boring. And cold.

This is the worst part of being a detective.

She ran a finger over the steel of the armour and wondered what it would be like to have to wear something like that. *Horrible*, she decided. *Must be really difficult to walk, all encased like that. Like a metal mummy. Oh dear . . . I wish I hadn't thought of that. Hurry up, Matthew – how long does it take to follow a . . .*

What was that?

A murmur of voices . . . from downstairs . . .

More guards? But why would guards be whispering to each other? Her detecting instincts at high pitch, Slightly crept to the top of the marble stairs and peered down. She was just in time to see a swirl of skirts disappearing out of sight, going in the direction of the lower galleries. The *Egyptian* galleries . . .

A shiver ran up Slightly's spine. She hesitated.

*It must be Miss Ponsonby and Professor Amberleigh –
mustn't it? – but what are they doing? What should I
do?* Then she realised her feet had already decided.
They were already taking her down the stairs.
Carefully, a step at a time, she worked her way as
silently as a shadow through the entrance hall and
into the first of the Egyptian galleries.

There was no one there, but in the room beyond
she thought she could hear something. Furtive
footsteps. The sound of a safety match striking.
A strange *gurgling* . . .

Slightly crept forward –

– and froze.

Floating in a blur of black, a glowing green shape
entered the room from the far door and moved
between the cases.

Slightly's heart juddered in her chest.

The Cambridge Mummy.

There was a swishing sound – and the mummy
disappeared! But the black shape around it . . . it
was still there . . . Slightly squinted . . . a shape in the
gloom . . . *almost like a* . . .

She reared back involuntarily as the mummy
suddenly reappeared, glowing green and eerie. Her
mind teemed with images – the green glowing
handprint on the Girton staircase – the ghostly

figure dancing on the lawn – Professor Amberleigh clutching the cursed necklace and pointing a shaking finger –

The mummy had stopped by one of the cases. There was a tiny click – the case opened – and in the dimness Slightly saw something being lifted out. She knew in her heart what it was. The mummy had come to claim its own. She heard the links of the cursed necklace chime softly together, and the gold and jewels glowed as if with an inner light.

Then something very peculiar happened.

The mummy reached into the case and put something back! A clatter of broken bits. Then it turned and as it did so, it stumbled as if over a long skirt, made a remarkably human tutting sound and began to abruptly bundle up the blackness. And underneath, it was wearing . . .

'Bloomers!'

Completely without meaning to, Slightly said the word out loud. The effect on the mummy was electrifying. With a shriek, it jumped into the air and threw itself at Slightly – she hit the floor with a thud, all the air knocked out of her lungs, and tried to roll away – the mummy seemed completely tangled up in folds of cloth – Slightly grabbed hold tightly. . .

There was a ripping sound, horribly loud in the echoing gallery, and Slightly found herself with a black hood in her hands, and a face she recognised just a few inches from her own.

CHAPTER NINE:
The Cambridge Mummy

Miss Ponsonby!

'*You're* the Cambridge Mummy?' gasped Slightly. '*You're* the one who's been smashing all those ancient things ... but that's *impossible!*'

Miss Ponsonby rose gracefully to her feet in spite of the tangling black robe. Slightly, still sprawled on the floor, could see clearly now that the green glow was from the picture of a mummy painted on the cloth.

Phosphorescent paint! she thought.
Of course! But ... why?

'But why?' Slightly said out loud.

'You're Egyptian! Why would you do this?'

'Do what?' said Miss Ponsonby. 'Do you really think I'm the vandal? I thought you were supposed to be clever!'

There was such a look of scorn on that lovely face that Slightly's temper snapped. She jumped up. 'Well?' she said, fists on hips. 'If you're not the vandal, why don't you tell me who *is*? And *this* time, you'd better answer my questions!'

Miss Ponsonby looked at her for a long moment, and then seemed to come to a decision. 'Do you really want to know who has been destroying the artefacts?' she whispered. 'Do you really want to solve the mystery, little lady Sherlock Holmes?'

'Yes, I do!'

'Then follow me. I will show you the answer. But you must come now – and silently! Not a sound.'

'But –' Slightly began, suddenly uncertain. 'But –'

Miss Ponsonby put her finger to her lips and repeated, 'Not a sound. Do you understand? Come with me. Unless you are too afraid, little girl.'

And then nothing short of an earthquake could have stopped her.

'Lead the way,' said Slightly Jones.

Miss Ponsonby hustled her down into the basement of the Museum, through a maze of underground corridors. Slightly tried to pay attention to the way but she had little chance.

'Hurry! Hurry!' Miss Ponsonby kept whispering urgently, looking back over her shoulder.

'Why?' called Slightly breathlessly. 'Who are we running away from?'

But she got no reply.

Down another corridor, a sharp turn to the right and they reached a door.

'In here . . .' Without ceremony, Miss Ponsonby shoved Slightly ahead of her into a cramped, gloomy room. 'Welcome to my kingdom.'

Slightly, panting, looked around.

Miss Ponsonby's kingdom was apparently used as a dumping ground for all the odd and awkwardly shaped things that the Museum just might need some day. It was also a sort of Lost and Found department – abandoned umbrellas, forgotten half-read novels, a forlorn baby's shoe – the flotsam and jetsam of countless Museum visitors had washed up here. Even sadder were the piles of damaged exhibits and unidentifiable debris on the shelving. And, incongruously, there was an enormous stone sarcophagus shoved awkwardly into one corner, leaving very little space for Miss Ponsonby's crowded worktable. Its heavy lid was raised using the Museum's portable hoist and there was Freddy Twist, jacketless and disheveled, lifting something out of it . . .

Slightly gasped. She'd seen that object before – she knew she had – in the photographs Miss Sprottle had shown them!

'Anubis!' she squeaked. 'The jackal with the tail – but it can't be . . . it was smashed . . . destroyed . . .'

Freddy spun round. His mouth dropped open. 'Gertrude! What the devil is *she* doing here?!' He looked down, appalled, at the statue in his hands and made as if to hide it behind his back.

'Drop that and I'll kill you,' said Miss Ponsonby. The velvety tones were completely gone. 'And stop calling me Gertrude. I told you – my name's Kepi.'

Slightly couldn't take her eyes off the statue.

'But I saw the broken bits!' she wailed in confusion. 'It was so smashed up there was practically nothing but dust left behind!'

Miss Ponsonby's grin was not very nice as she turned the key in the lock and put her back against the door.

'Indeed. So smashed up that if it hadn't been lying beside the label you'd never have known what it was. Think about it, clever little English girl. Piles of broken rubble beside a label that says 'This is a pot' or 'This is a statue'. Does that inevitably mean that the rubble is the remains *of* the pot or the statue? Couldn't it just be . . . rubble?'

Slightly's mouth dropped open, until she realised she looked like Freddy Twist and shut it again. It was a fiendishly cunning plot – so simple, so foolproof. And it explained why nothing was ever heard!

'Nothing was ever heard because there was nothing to hear!' she exclaimed. 'I didn't understand that . . . You made it *look* as if the artefacts had been destroyed, but all the while you were *stealing* them and leaving any old bits of smashed-up pottery or glass or stone in their place, so that no one would go looking for the real things. You could get away with it –'

'– as long as no one thought to look properly at what was left behind. Yes.' Miss Ponsonby smirked. 'The debris always came to me, of course, in my dingy little basement room. And I would seem so mournful and try my hardest but always I would fail to reconstruct the objects. Too bad. So sad. End of story. Meanwhile, my collection grew. I've been storing the artefacts right here, in the sarcophagus. With a lid weighing that much, nobody was going to go peeking inside on a whim.'

'Not without the portable hoist,' added Freddy proudly. 'That was *my* idea.'

'Given that the hoist is stored in my workroom it was hardly a leap of genius to think of *using* it,' said Miss Ponsonby scornfully. 'And now that I've acquired the final prize, the Mummy's Necklace, I'm going to put them all back.'

'Put them back?' said Slightly. For a moment she couldn't think what Miss Ponsonby meant.

'Return them to Egypt! Back where they belong.' She walked over to the crowded work table and lifted the lovingly wrapped parcels one by one.

'This is the hippo statue . . . this the papyrus . . . the canopic jars . . .' She gently stroked them as if they were delicate birds, roosting trustingly together. 'All my lovely things,' she murmured. 'Not long now, my dears, not long now.' She looked sidelong at Slightly with a sneer twisting her lovely mouth. 'And nobody suspected. Not even you, little lady. You were all too busy pretending *not* to believe the story of the curse and the walking dead that I made up – but you *did* believe – admit it, now, why don't you.'

The image of the mummy in the moonlight, dancing across the frosty Girton lawn, leapt into Slightly's mind. It must have shown in her face because Miss Ponsonby laughed.

'Pah – and you say *my* people are superstitious!'

Slightly couldn't stop her face growing red. She wanted to deny it – she wanted to argue – but Miss Ponsonby just snorted, turned her back and started to pull the black robe over her head.

'We've wasted enough time with this . . .'

'Oh, I say . . .' Freddy's eyes goggled as the bloomers were revealed in all their glory.

Miss Ponsonby looked at him wearily. 'Oh, for pity's sake, grow up.'

'Er. Righty-o. But look, what do we do with *her*? Now she's seen us, I mean. I mean, it changes things, doesn't it.'

Miss Ponsonby turned to Slightly.

'Yes . . . another problem to be solved . . .'

Slightly felt her heart clench. *I don't want to be solved!* she cried silently – and then she heard a familiar voice making a ruckus outside the room.

'Let *go* of me! *Ow!* That *hurt!*'

'*Now* what?!' spat Miss Ponsonby. She flung the black robe over the priceless artefacts on the table and then swore as the phosphorescent mummy painting landed face up and ghastly. 'Here!' She shoved Slightly bodily at Freddy and tried to rearrange the folds as the door opened . . .

CHAPTER TEN:
Celestial One

It was Professor Amberleigh. There was a strange, glazed expression on her face, and in her rigid grip, Matthew struggled. His collar was twisted right round, so that he was half-strangled and there was a vivid, red mark on the side of his face.

Slightly's thoughts raced. *What is the professor's part in all this? Is this another of her 'little episodes'?*

'This slave was *spying* on me,' Professor Amberleigh announced. Slightly could see how scared Matthew was – and felt even more frightened herself! 'Doesn't he know it is death to look on a queen without her leave? Even when I hit him, he wouldn't stop!' She lifted the squirming Matthew right off the floor and held him out at arm's length as if he were a bad smell.

'The slave will be dealt with, Celestial One,' Miss Ponsonby was saying. 'Leave him to me.'

The professor opened her hand and Matthew hit the floor in a heap. Slightly tried to go to him but Freddy stopped her by grabbing hold of her hair. The sudden pain made her gasp and brought tears to her eyes.

Professor Amberleigh turned at the sound. 'The Celtic slave girl!' she cried. 'Excellent. I won't need that other one now. Give her to me at once!'

Freddy shoved Slightly at the professor and hissed to Miss Ponsonby, 'What's the old bat doing *here*?! You said you were setting her up in the Egyptian galleries!'

Professor Amberleigh paid no attention to him. She sat down in the only chair with a regal flourish, closed her eyes and started to snore.

What's wrong *with her?* thought Slightly in confusion. And what was that smell? She was sure she remembered it from somewhere . . . but where? She turned to find Miss Ponsonby watching her closely.

'Ah, Miss Jones, it is so amusing to observe your little brain struggle to keep up,' she drawled. 'You wonder, do you not, what is going on?'

Trying to keep her voice from shaking, Slightly replied, 'Well? What *is* going on? What's the matter with the professor?'

'That dear, kind lady ... why, I've been grooming her to take the blame for destroying the artefacts, of course!'

And suddenly Slightly remembered where she'd smelled that sweet sickly scent before – wafting down the staircase in Girton College. 'You've been drugging her!'

Miss Ponsonby shrugged. 'I introduced her to the delights of the hubble bubble pipe, yes, and under its influence I told her wonderful tales. Tales to suit someone like her, someone who feels they don't have the power and respect they deserve. I told her the smoke of the pipe would give her access to her previous life – she would become part of the glory of ancient Egypt. Of course, I *could* have told her she'd been a slave or a peasant farmer's wife, but I think she might not have been so eager to embrace the idea then.

'No, I told her she'd been the most important woman in the land – a queen – a Celestial One – she swallowed *that* without difficulty. What a surprise.'

Freddy sniggered. 'She was so fuddled she started believing it even without the pipe – her "little episodes" you called them, Gert— I mean, Kepi. I thought she was going to blow everything yesterday, when she started seeing things right in front of everybody, and then she fell over like a big fat tree and I thought, "Crumbs, what do we do if she's, you know, dead?"'

Miss Ponsonby gave Freddy a withering look. 'Freddy?'

'Yes, Kepi?'

'Shut up.'

'Yes, Kepi.'

'And get the rest of the artefacts safely packed up,' she added, heading for the door.

'What? Why? I say! Where are you *going*?' Freddy looked panic-stricken.

'To get the hubble bubble pipe from the gallery, of course. We need to keep the old woman sweet, don't we.' And she strode out, shutting the door firmly behind her.

For a moment, they all just stared at it, except for Professor Amberleigh whose eyes were still shut. Then Slightly and Matthew both abruptly scrambled for the door handle . . .

Without opening her eyes, Professor Amberleigh caught hold of Slightly before she'd gone two steps. And Freddy hit Matthew with a flying tackle that flipped him, hard, against the wall. Slightly heard a horrible cracking sound as a bone snapped. Matthew's face went deathly white and he slid down the wall, cradling his left arm in his right with a cry of pain.

Freddy looked surprised. 'Well then ... that shows you, doesn't it ... no funny business round me then ...That goes for you too, missy,' he blustered when she tried to go to Matthew. But with Professor Amberleigh's fingers digging into her arm, Slightly was going nowhere.

Matthew tried to give her a reassuring grin, but it was more like a grimace.

After puffing out his scrawny chest at them, Freddy got on with wrapping up the last of the artefacts, his eyes flicking nervously towards the door every few seconds.

What should I do? thought Slightly wildly. *I don't know what to do!* Professor Amberleigh's grip on her was growing no weaker, Miss Ponsonby would return any second – and she had no plan!

Far too soon, she heard a scratching at the door. Freddy lit up like an eager puppy and rushed over to open it. Miss Ponsonby was back, laden down with a hubble bubble pipe.

It looked just like the one the caterpillar was smoking in the picture from Slightly's copy of *Alice's Adventures in Wonderland*. She remembered Granny reading it aloud to her as a bedtime story. Granny, who would be enjoying the service in the chapel at this very moment, sure that Slightly was only a few rows away. *I wish she would walk in right now.* But Granny didn't even know where she was. Nobody knew where she was. She had to blink hard to keep the tears back.

On spotting the pipe, the professor let go of Slightly and staggered over to the table with an eager cry. As Miss Ponsonby untangled the long tube and prepared to light the pipe, she took in Matthew's white face and limp arm. Slightly expected her to question Freddy, but she just shrugged. It meant nothing to her.

Soon the room began to fill with the sickly sweet smell of the smoke. The closer the pipe came to being ready, the more agitated and bad-tempered the professor became. She paced up and down, as far as the crowded room would allow.

'There! Look – he's doing it again. Staring at me, as if he had the right!'

Matthew quickly dropped his eyes. 'Weren't!' he muttered. 'Weren't staring at nobody.' But it was too late.

'Shall we punish him, Celestial One?' said Miss Ponsonby with a sly, sidelong glance at Matthew. 'Perhaps we should send him on ahead? To prepare for your arrival in the Afterlife?'

The professor pouted. 'I'm not sure I want an impertinent servant for all eternity. Besides, he's damaged now.' She pointed at Matthew's limp arm.

'Oh, he wouldn't be impertinent on the Other Side, my queen. He'd be nothing but respectful. Fix whatever's broken, too, I'd imagine. Crossing over has that effect. This is well known.'

''Ere – what are you on about?!' panted Matthew. 'I'm not crossing anything!' Slightly could see that he was in pain with every breath.

But the professor forgot all about him as Miss Ponsonby held out the pipe enticingly. 'Celestial One . . . ?'

The professor grabbed it, inhaled deeply, then let out a great cloud of the sickly smoke that made Slightly cough and cover her mouth.

'Join me, little slave.' Professor Amberleigh's voice had gone blurry round the edges. She seemed to be having trouble focussing on Slightly. 'Join me,' she repeated. 'Sit here and I will teach you the delights of the hubble bubble pipe.' She paused to suck again on the tube. Slightly could see the bubbles churn the coloured water in the glass jar and then subside, churn and subside. It was hypnotic, but all the while she was aware that Freddy was busily moving the wrapped artefacts from the table to the trolley waiting in the hallway, while Miss Ponsonby guarded the door against any more attempted breakouts.

'No thank you, Professor,' she said as politely as she could manage, while the professor waved the tube vaguely in her direction. She knew now how Miss Ponsonby had played on the older woman's ambitions and frustrations – how she had befuddled her mind with the smoke from the pipe – tricked her – set her up to take the blame for destroying the artefacts, when all the while they were being stolen. But what good was *knowing*, if Miss Ponsonby was still going to get away with it all?

I have to stop her, before it's too late! I have to – but how?!

There were only a very few parcels left to be removed. Time was running out . . .

She leaned close to the professor. 'Please, you must listen,' she whispered urgently. 'I'm Slightly Jones. I'm from *London* – don't you remember? I came to stay at your college for the Christmas holidays – you know, Girton College – you're a professor there. I'm not a slave! I came here freely, to solve the mystery of the Cambridge Mummy, but now they're keeping me against my will. Oh, don't you understand?'

The professor heaved a deep sigh. 'That is the lot of the slave, child. Sad, but inevitable. It is your fate. It is your destiny to serve me. Your great fortune . . . The gods led you here . . .'

'Nobody led me here! Well, no, that's not right . . . I guess you could say that Miss Ponsonby led me here. And you. At least, I followed you both here, which is pretty much the same thing. I think . . .'

The smoke was making Slightly's head swim. It was hard to form words. Think thoughts. Make plans . . .

She tried again. 'Miss Ponsonby has been lying to you – setting you up to take the blame for awful crimes – she's been drugging you.'

'Nonsense, child. Everyone knows that the smoke of the hubble bubble is benign. It soothes the spirit and clears the mind. I see and understand so much better when I have partaken. So much better.'

'No, Professor, it's just not true –' Slightly broke off with a gasp. The slap was so unexpected. Slightly cradled her cheek in her hand.

'You will call me Celestial One,' hissed Miss Amberleigh. 'I do not recognise this other title you use. I am a queen. You will treat me as such or you will pay the price.'

Slightly heard a soft chuckle behind her. It was Miss Ponsonby.

'Better do as she says,' she murmured from the doorway. 'She can get quite violent at this stage.'

Slightly remembered the bruises she'd seen on Miss Ponsonby's arms when they first met – and shivered.

'Do you wish me to remove the girl, Celestial One?'

'No – I want her. You can't have her,' said Professor Amberleigh. 'You can have the impertinent boy.'

The words were barely out of her mouth when, with more bravery than sense, Matthew made another dive for the door.

'Impertinent indeed,' said Miss Ponsonby as she caught hold of his shirt tails. 'Here, Freddy, take this. It needs safe storage, don't you think?' She shoved Matthew towards the back of the room.

'Eh? Oh, I see. Righty-o!' He took Matthew by his good arm and started to pull him past the work table, towards the sarcophagus . . .

'Stop – wait – what are you doing?!' cried Slightly.

'Oi!' squawked Matthew. He turned his head and frantically sank his teeth into Freddy's hand – Freddy screeched and let go – but Miss Ponsonby leaned forward and calmly gave Matthew a shove so that he toppled backwards and disappeared from view.

Slightly heard the nasty clunk of his head hitting the bottom of the sarcophagus. It must have stunned him because he didn't immediately jump up again, and Miss Ponsonby had time to knock the handle of the hoist – the lid slammed shut with a stony boom and Matthew was trapped . . .

'Time to go. And Freddy?'

'What?'

'Bring the hoist.'

With an unpleasant grin, Freddy did as he was told.

CHAPTER ELEVEN:
Entombed!

In the sudden silence, the key turning in the lock made an audible, ominous click. As the creaking of the trolley wheels and the sound of Miss Ponsonby's and Mr Twist's footsteps died away, Slightly couldn't hold back her tears any longer. She threw herself at the door and banged on it, sobbing.

This can't be happening! This can't be happening!

But it *was* happening, and crying wasn't going to help. *Get a hold of yourself, Slightly. You're just wasting time.*

And time was something they didn't have. Slightly wiped her face with her handkerchief and squared her shoulders.

Professor Amberleigh was swaying gently in her chair now, singing something in a whisper. Slightly caught a few words.

'. . . *deep and crisp and even . . . if thou knows't it, telling . . .*'

It was the Christmas carol *Good King Wenceslas*. The song seemed to strike the professor as funny, or perhaps it was something else completely, but she began to giggle, high-pitched and coy. The sound grated horribly on Slightly's nerves. All she could think about was Matthew. He was hurt and he was trapped – in the dark, in a small space where he would surely run out of air – he was buried alive. It was the dream she'd had, in real life this time – she could feel the darkness pressing down on him like a stifling blanket – the frantic way he was scrabbling at the sides, the lid – trying to scream but his throat so dry no sound came out –

'. . . *fails my heart, I know not how – I can go no longer . . .*' sang the professor, louder now.

Slightly flung herself at the lid of the sarcophagus but she was far too weak. Too light. Too little. She wished she were a big strong man. *Like Sherlock*

Holmes. Sherlock Holmes wasn't just smart, he was physically powerful as well. *He* could have man-handled the stone lid off the sarcophagus in a trice. *He* could have saved Matthew's life. She ran back to the door and pounded on it till her fists went numb, screaming as loudly as she could, 'Please! Someone – help! Help! Can anybody hear me? Is anybody there?'

But there was no one there. No one to hear her.

If only I were a big strong man . . .

She leaned her back against the door and looked round the room desperately for something . . . *any*thing . . . Her eyes fell on the humming professor and for a moment she stared at her without really seeing. Only very gradually did she begin to notice details. The professor's impressive height. Her broad shoulders. Her burly arms . . .

'Professor! Professor!' She rushed over and shouted in the woman's face. 'Listen to me! You've got to help!'

No effect. The professor waved her away vaguely as if she were a buzzing fly.

And then Slightly saw something on the table that made her heart jump. The policeman's smelling salts! No one had remembered to return the bottle to the constable and, like all the other Lost and

Found, it had ended up in Miss Ponsonby's workroom.

She grabbed the bottle and wrenched out the stopper. The harsh, acrid smell burned her throat and made her choke.

'Professor – help me – you must – wake up –'

Slightly shoved the bottle under the professor's nose. Professor Amberleigh reared back violently, cracking her skull smartly on the wall behind her. She snarled something incoherent but Slightly carried on waving the foul smell in her face again and again, until the professor staggered up and abruptly straight-armed her persecutor across the room. Slightly landed on the floor – the bottle went flying and smashed – and the sharp smell of ammonia cut through the sickly smoke from the pipe like a splash of cold water.

Eyes streaming, Slightly and Professor Amberleigh stared at one another.

'What . . . do you think . . . you're doing?' the professor rasped. 'Who *are* you?' She registered her surroundings. 'This is the Museum – *what am I doing here*?!'

Slightly flung herself at the professor's corsets and surprised them both by hugging her fiercely.

'Please – oh, please – there's no time – I'll explain

everything – but Matthew's trapped – he's going to die and I can't get the lid off –'

She dragged the professor over, pointing frantically at the massive sarcophagus.

Professor Amberleigh paled visibly. 'Some fool's *in there*?! But the lid's shut – there will be limited air! Is this some sort of silly Hide and Go Seek – don't you know how dangerous that is?! You should have called for help immediately!'

'I did, Professor. I tried. No one came. It's Christmas Eve – don't you remember? There's only us. There's only you and me.'

'And *you* are, again? No, never mind, tell me later. Well, there's no chance we can lift the lid, unless – I'm sure the Museum has some sort of hoist system . . .' She looked about, but Slightly shook her head.

'Freddy – Mr Twist – took it,' she said wearily.

'Ah. Freddy. That's just the sort of thoughtless thing he *would* do. Well, then, we must see if we can *push* . . .' Professor Amberleigh flexed her muscles, took a deep breath, put her hands against the lid and *heaved*.

Slightly eagerly added her own weight . . . but it was hopeless. The forces of inertia fought back, and won.

The professor straightened up, red-faced.

'Use your physics, Agnes,' she muttered, and shifted her position. 'Swivel . . .' She moved along the coffin and put her hands at the corner.

Please . . . please . . . thought Slightly. There was no room now for her to push, so she *stared* at the lid as if somehow she could make it move by sheer will. Nothing happened. Still nothing –

And then . . .

Slightly was sure she heard the twang of an exploding corset, just as the great weight of the lid began to shift. Little by little, with agonising slowness, stone grated against stone. Slightly's teeth ached with its screech.

She tried to see past the bulk of the professor, calling, 'Matthew! Matthew!' There was no answer. Professor Amberleigh took a deep breath and leaned to her task again.

The narrow gap widened – and widened – and then, woozy and white-faced, Matthew rose up out of the sarcophagus like a disheveled mummy and mumbled, 'What *happened*?!'

'Matthew!' cried Slightly. 'You're alive – you're alive!'

'I'm not so sure . . .' he groaned. 'Oww – no – let me get out myself –'

One-armed, with infinite care, he climbed out of the sarcophagus and leaned against it, squinting at them.

'Blimey, I don't half feel rough. Either of you ladies got any smelling salts?'

He looked confused when Slightly began to laugh a little hysterically. She settled him carefully on the chair and wished desperately that she knew more about first aid. He really did look awful.

'You certainly appear to require medical attention, young man,' said Professor Amberleigh, sounding more than a little disapproving. She strode over to the door and wrenched at the doorknob vigorously but without success. 'Why is this door locked? I really cannot understand why no one has come to investigate the noise we've been making.' She turned and glared at the two of them, as if it were somehow their fault.

'There's nobody here,' grunted Matthew. 'I tailed the last guard to the door, and he was leaving as fast as his cowardly feet would take him. I was coming back for Slightly when you nabbed me.'

'Don't be ridiculous, young man. I've never "nabbed" anyone in my life. I can only think you are suffering from some sort of asphixiatory hallucination. However, if your information on the staff is correct, then we must seek reinforcements from elsewhere.'

She stepped back and surveyed the problem.

'There.' And she pointed.

There was a fanlight over the door. It was so dirt-encrusted Slightly hadn't even noticed it, but 'Right,' said the professor. 'We'll have *that* open.'

She dragged a chair across the room and clambered up onto it. The fanlight may have been sealed for years, but it didn't stand a chance against a determined lady professor like Agnes Amberleigh. With a screech, it clunked forward to its full extent. Even so, the space was less than a foot high.

Matthew took a deep breath, and then seemed to immediately regret it. Nevertheless he stood up, only wobbling a little.

'Right. Stand back. This is a job for somebody who's had experience in creative entering and exiting . . .'

'Matthew, you're in no state to be entering or exiting *any*thing. I'll do it,' said Slightly as firmly as she could manage. 'Ladies first, remember?'

'Come on, girl,' boomed the professor. 'Better out than in!'

Before she could think of any answer to that, Slightly found herself hoisted up to the fanlight and shoved unceremoniously through it. She tried to grab hold but her fingers slipped and she scraped gracelessly down, hitting the floor hard, jarring her teeth together, twisting her ankle and collapsing into a heap.

'Slightly? Slightly?' She heard Matthew's muffled voice through the wood of the door.

'Young woman!' Professor Amberleigh boomed through the fanlight.

Slightly groaned, dragged herself over to the keyhole and put her mouth to it.

'I'm fine,' she whispered urgently. 'I'm fine. There . . . there's no key. I'm going to find the key, and let you out.'

'Slightly! No! It's not safe – you mustn't . . .' hissed Matthew.

But she was already on her way.

CHAPTER TWELVE:
Race Against Time

Slightly was already limping with grim determination down the corridor, going . . .

Where AM I going?

It had seemed so important to get out of that horrible room but now that she was loose in a sprawling labyrinth of basement passageways and storerooms, she realised she hadn't a clue what came next.

Get out of room – good. Get caught and put back in – bad. Find key and release Matthew and the professor – good. Don't find key and release nobody – bad.

That was as far as she'd got. It was hardly an elegant, detailed plan of attack. Nobody would want to write it down in admiration, the way Dr Watson did for Sherlock Holmes.

The corridor she was in ended at a T-junction. Slightly hesitated, peering right, then left. How could she tell which way to go? Both directions looked identical – dimly lit passageways, with stone flagged floors and walls painted a peculiarly unattractive pea-soup colour. This was the part of the building the public was never expected to visit. There were no helpful signs or labels.

Slightly stood for a long moment, just staring straight ahead, her mind spinning furiously, trying to work out where she was, what was the layout of the floors above ... *Just like the game of Hide and Go Seek I was playing with Matthew – could it really only have been this afternoon?* she was thinking – when suddenly she realised that on one side of her face, she could feel a cold breeze ...

Somewhere, down to the left, a door had been opened to the outside.

Slightly scurried towards the source of the draft. The corridor led her to an exit at the very back of the Museum. The gaslight flickered as an icy wind blew in through the open door. And Slightly could see someone outside moving about against the darkness.

Two someones.

'Careful, you fool! That pot's worth a sight more than you are.'

'Sorry, Gertrude – I mean, Kepi.'

Slightly crept closer, keeping to the shadows. Empty packing cases lined the passageway and she slid in behind a stack of them. From her hiding place, she could see the trolley piled with bundles – all the artefacts they'd believed lost, shattered beyond repair – standing in the doorway. Out in the alley, she could see the horse and cart, with Miss Sprottle's bicycle sticking incongruously up. Freddy was taking parcels from the trolley and handing them up to Miss Ponsonby to pack in the straw.

'Do we ditch the bicycle?' he was saying. 'You can't just peddle back to Girton now, as if nothing had happened, and wait for everybody to blame the old woman. We need a new plan – you'd be far better coming away with me on the train to Liverpool.' He sounded pathetically hopeful. 'And then on to Egypt, don't you know!'

Slightly heard Miss Ponsonby snort. 'I've *made* a new plan, but you're not in it. You get me and the parcels onto the train then *you* take the bicycle and go to . . . anywhere you like.'

'Oh, Gertrude – you don't mean that!' Slightly saw that Freddy had paused with a parcel in his hands, held up as if he were making an offering to a goddess.

'Hurry up – I want to be gone,' Miss Ponsonby snapped.

'Say you don't mean it!' insisted Freddy, keeping the parcel out of her reach like a badly behaved little boy.

Miss Ponsonby sighed. 'Oh, all right,' she said grudgingly. 'You can come with me – only hurry up!'

Slightly slumped against the wall. She didn't want them to be getting along! Thoughts racketed around her mind. What should she do? She *couldn't* just let them drive away . . . For one mad moment, she imagined stepping out from the shadows and demanding, 'You there! Stop in the name of the law!' Fortunately, common sense kicked in before she gave herself away. *Get help, Slightly!* But first what she needed to do was get *out*!

What she needed, was a distraction.

With her heart pounding so loudly she was afraid they would hear it, Slightly crept forward – and slid the nearest parcel off the trolley. Cradling it in her arms she scuttled back into the shadows and hid it in the boxes behind the door. Twice more she tiptoed out, when Freddy's back was turned and Miss Ponsonby was concentrating on packing straw around her treasures, to steal from the thieves – hoping and praying all the while that Miss Ponsonby knew *exactly* how many artefacts there should be – and Freddy Twist *didn't*. For what felt like forever, the two conspirators went about their work in a tense silence. All that could be heard was the occasional snortle from the horse or shifting of its hooves, Freddy's heavy breathing, and the rustle of straw as Miss Ponsonby packed each load away, until . . .

'Well?' she suddenly snapped. 'Have you fallen asleep? Give me the next one!'

'What? What are you on about?' grunted Freddy, stretching his back. 'There isn't a next one. That's it.'

Miss Ponsonby stared. 'Don't be ridiculous. Where's the hippo – and the wooden boat – and the statue of Bastet, the cat goddess – you've left them behind! Didn't I tell you to bring *everything*? How could you be so useless?!'

'I didn't leave anything behind!' Freddy stuck out his non-existent chin. 'You've miscounted.'

Quarrels among thieves! thought Slightly, hugging

herself nervously in the shadows. *Just what the detective ordered . . .*

Miss Ponsonby gave Freddy a look that should have turned *him* into a mummy but still he insisted, 'If you don't believe me, go and see for yourself.'

Miss Ponsonby spat out an Egyptian word that Slightly could tell was rude and climbed down over the side of the cart. Freddy automatically stepped forward to give her a hand, but she pushed it away.

'They were all there, IN a pile, OUTSIDE the door, IMPOSSIBLE to miss,' she muttered darkly. 'If you paid more attention to the *extremely simple* tasks I give you, and less attention to my legs . . .' Slightly pressed herself even further into the shadows as Miss Ponsonby strode angrily past.

'And these are the people who think they're masters of the world,' she was snarling to herself. The slightest glance to the side and she would have seen . . .

But as far as Miss Ponsonby was concerned, Slightly and Matthew and Professor Amberleigh had been dealt with. One way or another. She carried on, unaware of the cowering detective a few feet away.

Slightly's heart was jumping in her chest like a wild thing.

One down, one to go.

If she could just get Freddy to leave, even for a moment. But Freddy showed no sign of budging. He leaned against the cart and lit a cigarette, muttering crossly to himself between puffs. Time was ebbing fast . . .

Slightly pushed her hands into her pockets in frustration – and her fingers closed on the sixpence Granny had given her to put in the offering plate at Evensong. Without hesitating, she drew back her arm and threw it with all her might, down the alleyway, into the darkness. The coin hit the cobbles with a satisfying clatter.

'Eh? What? Who's there?' Freddy nearly swallowed his cigarette in panic, but for one awful moment it looked to Slightly as if he *still* wasn't going to shift. He just stood there dithering, peering anxiously down the alleyway in the direction of the noise and then back into the Museum, as if hoping Miss Ponsonby was about to return and take command.

Go and look! Go and look! Slightly held her breath . . . Freddy took a few steps away from the door . . . all his attention was focused down the alley . . . Slightly crept forward . . . and ran!

With every step she expected to hear Freddy shout, 'Hey! You!' and come pounding after her. The alley spilled out onto a side street which fed into Trumpington Road. Now she fled in earnest. Without her coat or hat, the night air bit hard. The moon looked down, white and indifferent as Slightly's breath streamed behind her, great pale puffs in the freezing air. The pretty sparkle of frost on the pavement and cobbles was a sinister, slippery trap – she skidded and almost fell again and again, but she didn't dare slow down. The cold air hurt her lungs and her ankle ached from where she'd twisted it falling out of the fanlight, but she couldn't let any of that stop her. She had to keep going.

It was impossible to get lost on the route from the Fitzwilliam to King's College – of course it was impossible! It was practically a straight run, no sharp turns or corners . . .

Wasn't it? Shouldn't she be there by now?

What if it's too late? What if everyone had gone home and no one had even noticed that she and Matthew were missing? It was impossible to judge how long they'd spent at the Museum. It felt like forever.

But then, at last, the chapel loomed into sight, and for one terrible moment she thought she'd lost her mind. Nothing had changed! The lights still shone from the tall windows, the crowds still stood about the door – it was as if no time had passed *at all*!

But that's impossible! All the things that had happened . . . Then,

'Lovely service, wasn't it?' she heard someone on the edge of the crowd comment to his neighbour, and it all became clear.

Evensong was over. Those who had attended were simply enjoying each other's company before returning to their own homes, their own Christmas celebrations.

Slightly dithered at the edge of the throng, panting and desperate. She couldn't see her friends anywhere. *They can't have gone without me, without us – they just CAN'T have. But where are they?*

How could she find *anyone* amongst all these people?

And then she saw him – Mr Entwhistle – the human heron, taller by a head than anyone else. And where Mr Entwhistle was, Miss Sprottle would surely be, and Miss Forth, and Granny. Especially Granny. *She* would know what to do . . .

For the second time that night Slightly found herself weaselling through the crowd in its Christmas finery. It had been so easy when all she had to do was get one small choirboy out of trouble. But this time, when so much was at stake, it was like pushing through treacle. She zigged and zagged, desperately trying to keep her general direction straight towards her friends, but long skirts threatened to tangle her up – gentlemen's canes tried to trip her – the way was blocked at every turn by fabric and fur.

'Let me pass – please – oh, please –'

And then something miraculous happened. The crowd parted, so suddenly that Slightly would have crashed to her knees if someone familiar hadn't caught her up in a big hug.

'It *was* you!' cried Granny. 'We were sure you and Matthew had sat further back in the chapel and we'd meet up again at the end, but then I thought I saw you, running down the street, and then you disappeared in the scrum.'

'And then all we had to do was head towards the ladies squealing and the gentlemen jumping as if someone had just poked them in the, er, ribs,' added Mr Entwhistle cheerfully.

'Heavens – where's your coat?!' asked Miss Sprottle.

But Granny brushed the question of coats aside. She could tell that something important was wrong. 'What is it, Slightly? Where have you been? What has happened?'

Slightly was gasping so hard her lungs burned, and the words only came out in disconnected bursts.

'Hurry – Ponsonby – mummy – alley – behind Museum – and Freddy – not smashed – STOLEN!'

Her friends just stared at her.

'I'm sorry, dear, but I don't quite . . .' began Miss Forth, when Granny shook her head firmly and took charge.

'Mr Entwhistle, get us a cab,' she barked, starting to plough her way energetically through the crowd.

'Er, yes, of course, but – where to?!' yelped Mr Entwhistle.

'To the Fitzwilliam Museum, of course!'

Slightly had barely caught her breath enough to tell them what had been happening before the cab was approaching the Fitzwilliam.

'I can't believe it! I can't believe it!' Mr Entwhistle was repeating, while Miss Sprottle's hair positively exploded from its pins. 'The rotter!' she exclaimed. 'The . . . the *hussy*!'

'Look! There they are!' cried Slightly.

Miss Ponsonby was easing the cart out into Trumpington Street with Freddy hunched on the seat beside her. The moonlight glinted off the jewels of the Mummy's Necklace she wore proudly round her neck. She was driving as if the cart was full of glass eggs, but as Slightly's cry reached her ears, she snatched up the whip and slashed the horse with it.

The horse screamed and half-reared, its hooves slipping on the icy cobbles – the cart slewed sideways and teetered on two wheels – for one horrible moment it looked as if it was about to overturn and smash all the Museum's treasures in earnest. Freddy Twist, with a scream as loud as the horse's, leapt out and ran away. Miss Ponsonby wrenched the bicycle over the side, threw herself onto it and disappeared down an alleyway, peddling furiously.

'Stop her!' bellowed Mr Entwhistle. 'She's stolen the necklace!'

But Miss Sprottle cried even louder, 'Stop her – she's stolen my *bicycle*!'

CHAPTER THIRTEEN:
Mistress Trenchant's Prediction

Miss Sprottle's bicycle was discovered on Boxing Day by the Cambridge police, abandoned and forlorn in a hedge on the outskirts of town. But there was no sign of Miss Ponsonby or Freddy Twist – or the infamous Mummy's Necklace. It had vanished, taking its curse with it. In the Fitzwilliam Museum, the undead walked no more, and the guards returned to their duties with relief.

'Do you think Miss Ponsonby will get the necklace back to Egypt?' Slightly asked Granny.

But Granny didn't answer.

Professor Amberleigh was not going to be returning to Girton College in the new term. She was on extended leave, due to what was being described as 'exhaustion from overwork'. (When they heard this, some of the gentlemen professors nodded knowingly at each other. Clearly, ladies really shouldn't try to push their way into the world of the university. 'They're not built for it,' they told each other solemnly. 'It just overheats their feminine brains.')

Matthew was ensconced in the college Infirmary, where he was being enthusiastically waited on by Miss Forth. The doctor diagnosed a broken collar bone.

'Four weeks to heal, another four after that and you'll never know it happened,' he announced cheerfully. 'Keep that left arm in the sling, of course. And for internal application, I prescribe plenty of beef tea, roast mutton, rabbit, calves' feet – what about a nice calves' head jelly? – I'm sure all these lovely ladies will be delighted to whip up anything light and easily digested along those lines.'

'Blimey,' said Matthew. 'I've died and gone to heaven!'

As soon as Miss Forth said he was fit enough,

Miss Sprottle arrived with her notebook and propelling pencil at the ready, to 'consult' him on London slang. When Slightly asked him just what that involved, he grinned sheepishly and said, 'Mostly I try to keep her off of expressions ladies shouldn't ought to know. She's cussed persistent though!'

During *her* visits to the Infirmary, Slightly took every opportunity to bring up how she'd saved him from a terrible fate. Well, she and Professor Amberleigh.

'It's a dangerous business, this detecting,' she told him solemnly. 'It's ever so easy to get out of your depth. Leave it to the experts, that's the thing . . .'

And then Matthew would throw pillows at her until she ran away giggling.

During the rest of their time in Cambridge, the town was quiet, waiting for the students to return. Slightly explored it with Miss Forth and Granny. She looked about at the beautiful, venerable buildings and the quiet river and the pale winter sky, and she couldn't stop the smile from spreading across her face.

I love Cambridge, she thought.

Just before it was time to go home to London, one more thing happened that Slightly was to remember for a long time to come. The head of Girton, known as the mistress, returned to the college, and when she was settled she invited Miss Sprottle and her guests for afternoon tea in her suite of rooms.

Slightly put on her best puffed-sleeve blouse and blacked her shoes and brushed her hair a hundred times. She looked in the mirror, hoping for a miracle, but she didn't really look any different. Miss Forth, as always, was already effortlessly immaculate, and Granny just looked like Granny. Miss Sprottle, on the other hand, kept jamming in more and more hairpins as they walked along the long arched corridors, not noticing the ones she dislodged. She seemed more than a little nervous as she knocked on the mistress's door.

'Enter!'

If Slightly had had to say what she thought the mistress of Girton College would look like, she probably would have imagined someone like Professor Amberleigh. Someone tall and imposing, with a cut-glass voice and arrogant eyes and extremely tight corsets.

She would *not* have imagined someone like Mistress Julia Trenchant.

'Good to see you, Mellifluous. How's the book

coming along? Miss Tonic – Miss Forth – please come in.'

Mistress Trenchant was a small woman with glossy, chestnut-coloured hair piled high on her head like a shiny conker. Her gown was a soft, mossy-green material that flowed down to embroidered slippers. She had a round face with rosy cheeks, and the bright blue eyes of an inquisitive baby. She looked harmless and simple, yet somehow Slightly knew for certain that neither of these things were true.

'And this must be the young lady whose quick thinking helped both the college and the Museum.' Mistress Trenchant smiled at her. 'What is your name?'

Slightly bobbed a curtsey. 'Slightly Jones, ma'am.'

'Well, Miss Jones, I'd like to thank you. Without your assistance, a number of valuable artefacts would have been lost from our lovely Museum – indeed from our country entirely – and we might never have solved the mystery of their fate. I hear from Miss Sprottle that all of the stolen items have been put back where they belong.'

'Well, yes, though . . .' Slightly caught Granny's warning look and stopped abruptly.

Mistress Trenchant seemed to be hiding a smile. 'I believe Miss Jones has something to say? Please do not worry, Miss Tonic. I am quite capable of looking after myself in a debate. You were about to say, Miss Jones?'

'Well, ma'am, I was just going to say that they — the, um, artefacts — they weren't really ours to begin with.' Miss Sprottle gave a muffled gasp, but Slightly ploughed on. 'I know it was wrong of Miss Ponsonby to do . . . what she did . . .'

'You mean, stealing from the Fitzwilliam Museum?' said Mistress Trenchant. 'Deluding one of my staff, encouraging a dangerous addiction, and conspiring to have that unfortunate woman branded as a criminal? Putting yourself and the young gentleman in danger of your lives? Not to mention the injury inflicted on him by her associate. I should certainly think that those actions were "wrong", as you say. And this is without raising the question of having fooled *me*. She *did* fool me, Miss Jones, completely. I don't like being anyone's dupe.'

Slightly had no problem believing that! She gulped and said, 'Yes, ma'am. I mean no, ma'am. Except that I don't think she entirely saw it like that. I'm not saying she was nice, because I don't think she was. But as far as stealing goes, didn't we steal the things from her country in the first place? Which would mean that by stealing them *she* was just putting them back where they belonged. Ma'am.'

The mistress looked at Slightly steadily. 'If your – and Miss Ponsonby's – premise is correct, than your conclusion would be too. Though you might find, if you give the matter further thought, that your premise is a little . . . simple. I suggest that you do just that – think some more – and then, when you return to us in not so many years, we will speak again.'

Slightly wasn't sure she'd understood properly. 'When I return . . .?'

Mistress Trenchant smiled. She had a smile that made you want to smile back. 'Yes, Miss Jones. When you return. I may have been wrong about Miss Ponsonby, but I am willing to hazard that I am not wrong about you. When you are ready for Girton College, it will be ready for you. And in the meantime, ladies, may I offer you some tea?'

⌒ ❀ ⌒

Time passed. The students, both male and female, came back to Cambridge, and Slightly, Granny and Miss Forth returned to Limpopo House, to a warm welcome from the gentlemen lodgers and Cleopatra the cat.

It's good to be home, thought Slightly.

And then, suddenly, the season changed. Almost

between one day and the next, it turned into spring. The dirty grey slush that was London's version of snow disappeared. Flower sellers peddled bunches of primroses and violets and blackthorn blossom. And Slightly exploded into the kitchen, covered in mud.

'What in heaven's name . . . !' cried Granny.

'Miss Forth and I have been practising our bicycling in the park and I only came off three times! And Miss Forth wouldn't have come off at all if some boys hadn't started chasing her and saying rude things about her bloomers. And then Matthew chased them and then he caught one and we had to go and stop them fighting. It was really thrilling!'

'Ah,' said Granny, sounding resigned. 'Bicycling.'

She would probably have said more, but just then there was a double knock on the front door.

'Ah. There. That'll be the police come to arrest you all for disturbing the peace.'

'You know it's the postman – he always knocks twice!' said Slightly, dancing round the table, completely unabashed. 'I'll go.'

'You most certainly will not,' retorted Granny. 'You're in no fit state to be seen by postmen *or* police! Go to your room and get into clean clothes. *I* will go to the door.'

Slightly skipped along behind Granny and

started up the stairs. She heard the front door open but instead of their usual postman's familiar voice, someone much younger piped up.

'Telegram delivery, ma'am. Does a Mr Reginald Westerly live here?'

Slightly stopped short, her detective's curiosity on high alert, and looked down between the railings.

It was a telegraph messenger boy. He was out of breath from running as fast as possible all the way from the Post Office.

'A telegram?' exclaimed Granny. 'For Mr Westerly? Oh dear, I hope it's not bad news.'

'I brought a blank form, in case there's to be an answer,' panted the boy. He pulled a piece of paper out of his pocket and held it out.

'Oh . . . yes . . . thank you. If you'll just wait a moment . . .'

'I'll tell him, Granny,' Slightly called down. She hurried along to Mr Westerly's combination bedroom and studio, and knocked on the door. Mr Westerly stuck his head out. His moustache was shiny and turned up at the ends, a sign that his painting was going well. Slightly hated to interrupt, but a telegram – it could be important!

Mr Westerly looked alarmed when she told him, and they both hurried down to the kitchen, passing the messenger boy kicking his heels and whistling carelessly in the hallway.

Granny handed Mr Westerly the telegram, poured him a cup of tea and waited wordlessly.

What can it be? thought Slightly anxiously. *Is it bad news? Good news?*

It was the work of a moment to read, but Mr Westerly seemed to be having trouble understanding exactly what the words meant.

'It's from my good friend, Peter March – a most talented artist. He is living in Montmartre, in Paris, and he seems to be in trouble, but with so few words at his disposal, he has been most cryptic. Most . . . confusing!'

He handed the telegram to Slightly, and tried to spruce up his moustache which had dropped alarmingly. Slightly read aloud:

'Maria kidnapped. Dare tell no one. Ransom demand signed Hidden City. Afraid.'

Slightly's brain began to buzz. *Hidden City! Kidnapping! Ransom!*

'What does it mean, Mr Westerly?' asked Granny. 'Who is Maria?'

Mr Westerly stared at her in distress. 'I don't know! We've . . . we've lost touch since he moved to France. Poor chap, poor chap, you can hear how desperate he is – I must answer him immediately. I must send him a return telegram.' He reached for the reply form and then stared at it helplessly.

'What shall I do? Six pence to send twelve words – what can I possibly say in twelve words? What should I tell him to do?'

Mr Westerly looked at Slightly. Slightly pulled out her silver propelling pencil, and looked at Granny. Granny tried to look stern, but failed miserably. Slightly Jones, detective-in-training, pushed her unruly hair out of her eyes, smeared the mud on her cheek a little further, turned to Mr Westerly and handed him her pencil.

'Tell him this . . .' she said, and as she dictated, Mr Westerly wrote out the telegram in his beautiful copperplate handwriting:

'Do nothing. Help is on the way. We will take the case.'

TO BE CONTINUED IN
The Case of the Hidden City

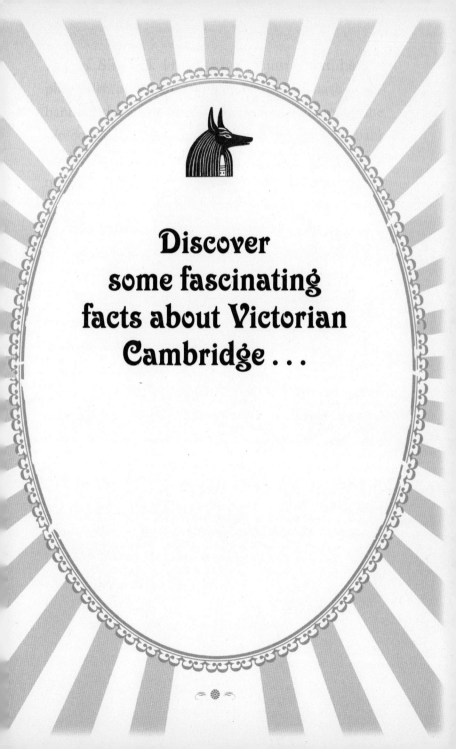

Discover
some fascinating
facts about Victorian
Cambridge . . .

Did you know...

...Girton College has its own mummy?

Her name is Hermione and she was bought for the college in 1911 for the princely sum of £20. Hermione is a portrait mummy, where the face of the person is painted on a wooden board and wrapped up with the strips of cloth. There is an inscription on her portrait which reads *Hermione Grammatike* which can be translated as *Hermione the literary lady* – so Girton was certainly a good place for her to end up!

...that Victorian manner books gave warnings to men with moustaches?

'It requires some expertness and practice for a man with a moustache to take soup in a perfectly inoffensive manner. The accomplishment is worth some trouble.' *Mrs Humphry's Manners for Men,* 1897.

. . . how to make smelling salts?

As early as the 1600s, people were using shavings from deer horns and hooves to make an ammonia solution. The sharp smell, wafted under the fainting victim's nose, was pretty much guaranteed to get a reaction.

. . . that newspapers published advice to lady cyclists?

In 1895 the *New York World* printed a list of Don'ts for women on bicycles, which included these wise words:

❀ Don't go to church in your bicycle costume.

❀ Don't wear a garden party hat with bloomers.

❀ Don't chew gum. Exercise your jaws in private.

❀ Don't [go out] without a needle, thread and thimble.

❀ Don't allow dear little Fido to accompany you

❀ Don't discuss bloomers with every man you know.

❀ Don't try to ride in your brother's clothes "to see how it feels."

❀ Don't scream if you meet a cow. If she sees you first, she will run.

... how to make an ivy ribbon?

Ivy ribbons were popular Christmas decorations in Victorian times. If Slightly can make them, then so can you!

1. You'll need some ivy leaves, a strip of cloth or newspaper a bit narrower than the leaves, a needle and green thread.

2. Place an ivy leaf so the tip overlaps the top of the ribbon and stitch up from under the ribbon. One stitch will do it.

3. Lay another leaf on the ribbon so it covers the stitch in the first one. Sew one stitch up from under the ribbon as before.

4. Stitch on more leaves – you can always add more cloth or newspaper. Once finished, turn the ribbon over and secure any loose threads with sticky tape.

There you have it, a real, homemade ivy ribbon – perfect for a present-day Christmas!

Cambridge Quiz

Test your knowledge of Victorian and modern-day Cambridge with these questions . . .

True or False:

a) Miss Sprottle was right when she said that women would become fully part of Cambridge University very soon – certainly before the beginning of the new 20th century.

b) The effigy of the lady on a bicycle was hung out in the town centre in 1897, in protest against the idea of women being given degrees.

c) In Victorian times, some people thought that too much studying would make a female's brain overheat.

Mr Entwhistle tried to send Freddy Twist to a chemist shop across the road from the Fitzwilliam Museum to get smelling salts. If you look today you'll see it's still there, with a fine big shield over the door that says 'G. Peck & Son Ltd. Dispensing Chemists Est. 1851'. If you ask a modern policeman for smelling salts, however, you may very well get some strange looks.

If you visit the Fitzwilliam Museum today, can you find the following?

❋ a statue of Anubis – a god shaped like a jackal with a spectacularly long tail
❋ an Egyptian necklace – without a curse!
❋ a suit of armour that Slightly might have hidden behind
❋ a papyrus from the *Book of the Dead*
❋ a silver trowel with the original floor plan of the Fitzwilliam Museum engraved on the blade

The Christmas Eve Evensong service (which Slightly and Matthew missed) at King's College Chapel later became the world-famous Festival of Nine Lessons and Carols. The carols and readings have been recorded and broadcast since 1928 and now millions of people tune in every year on Christmas Eve.

Do you know who Pegasus was?

What does the Egyptian name Kepi mean?

To find the answers to these questions and learn more about her other books, visit the author's website:
www.joanlennon.co.uk

A SLIGHTLY JONES MYSTERY
The Case of the London Dragonfish

Slightly Jones has red hair, too many freckles and a flyaway temper, but she's not going to let that stop her from becoming the next Sherlock Holmes . . .

A precious fossil is about to be presented to Queen Victoria at the Natural History Museum in London. But when the exhibit goes missing, the finger points to an innocent man. Slightly Jones won't let the real culprit get away with it – and with the help of Granny Tonic, Slightly is determined to save the day.

A SLIGHTLY JONES MYSTERY
The Case of the Hidden City

Paris in the springtime – the City of Art
and Artists at its loveliest! But it would seem that
there is a sinister side to all this beauty. Rumours
of a mysterious organisation called The Hidden City
are rife, and when not just paintings, but artists
and their models too, start to disappear,
no one knows what to think.

Out of her country for the first time,
Slightly Jones soon finds herself out
of her depth as well. Will she be
lost forever under the
streets of Paris?